THORN

ANNA BURKE

Bywater
BOOKS

Ann Arbor

For Tiffany
May you always be a thorn in my side

She smelled it, sharp and bitter on the wind.

The pack smelled it, too.

Blood, and another smell—a smell she had not scented in years, not this far north. She padded through the woods; the pack ranged behind and ahead and to either side, white shapes against the blue-white drifts.

Tracks.

Fresh.

Leather, horse, lynx, wolf, elk, bear, sweat, blood, piss, ale, wool, metal, grain, smoke.

She raised her head, nostrils flared, turning from side to side for any sounds beyond the creaking pines.

There.

Downwind, but it didn't matter. Not for this game. A faint jingle. A creak that was not bark on bark. A cough that did not belong to cat or elk.

The old hate quickened.

The pack tightened around her.

Red tongues lolled.

Breath steamed.

Winter bared her teeth.

Chapter One

They say the Huntress rides out when the sun is at its farthest and Winter has her jaws buried deep in the heart of the warm, green world. In the mountain valleys, they swear you can hear her hounds on the knife's edge of the wind, howling down the peaks in a spray of teeth. The Huntress rides behind them mounted on a great white bear with a horn of silver and bone at her lips and a spear cut from the living heart of a mountain pine at her side. No beast can stand before her charge, and every northern child knows that the Huntress stalks the snows, looking for the lost, the unwary, and the bold alike.

So they say, and so the story wanders farther and farther from the truth as the seasons turn, save for the one place time doesn't touch and cold preserves.

Her keep lies atop the tallest mountain, where the snow never melts and spring cannot bear to shine its yellow light, and the only thing that blooms on those chill stones is the white of the winter rose. They say the veins of that flower run red with heart's blood, and that to pluck but a single blossom from that mountaintop is to bring the wrath of Winter herself down on you.

I would know, for I have felt the prick of those thorns.

My father came down from the mountain three days after my seventeenth birthday. I remember the smell of snow, and the dark needles of the pines lying stark and cool against the blinding white of the drifts.

His horse was more ice than hair when it stumbled into the clearing where our cottage stood, steam freezing in clouds around its muzzle and icicles clinking as it walked. Frost rimed my father's beard, and behind him on a vast sledge were stacked the frozen pelts of wolves and elk and mountain lions, a lord's ransom in winter fur.

He rode in alone, and my sisters ran out to catch him as he slid from the horse while I stayed in the doorway, knuckles white against the red of my skirt as the weak sun made its way down over the rooftops and I counted the shadows of the hunters who had not returned.

I should have run to him. I should have rested my warm hands on his frozen face, but I had felt misfortune's shadow fall over me too many times before. I knew, even as the wealth of the forest promised new beginnings and an end to old debts, that Winter was upon us.

"Rowan, the door."

I put down my spindle with a groan, gathering the gray wool into my basket and tucking it back underneath my chair. My younger sister rolled her eyes.

"You could pretend to be sick again," Aspen suggested.

"That excuse is wearing as thin as my boots. Besides. Then they'll be saying I'm weak as well as odd."

Aspen faked a delicate cough and rolled her eyes at Juniper, our youngest sister. "Well, you've hardly gone out of your way to change their minds about the odd part," she said.

I swallowed the bitterness and pushed down the memory of home—our real home in the city, not this thatch and timber prison surrounded by sentinel pines and hardwoods—and forced a smile.

"You could at least pretend to like him, then," Aspen said, her tone softening. "It's not as awful as all that."

I lowered my eyes, hating myself for the rush of shame that

flushed my face. Aspen was right, of course. At least we had this place, an oversight, a scrap of land so far removed from civilization that my father's creditors had not even bothered to assess its value. At least I had the luxury of a house to hate.

"Pretend to like Avery?" This time the smile felt more real.

"He just hates that you can read and he can't. Which, by the way, you might try not reminding him."

"If he never opened his mouth that would be so much easier," I said, my hands checking my hair despite myself. It was no use. It fell heavily around my shoulders, thicker and coarser than Aspen's, and as unruly as a mountain goat's.

Aspen, with her red lips and dark hair, was by far the beauty of the family, and the knowledge was not lost on her. Even Juniper, though she had yet to master the simultaneous use of all of her limbs—a condition that made itself apparent in symptomatic shards of shattered pottery—shared Aspen's heart-shaped face and gentle curves. Where my father's coastal blood had tempered my mother's wilder features in my sisters, I alone looked like I belonged here in the tiny village of Three Elms.

The irony cut deep.

"You could try doing something besides talking."

Her words doused any good mood I had managed to salvage. "Keep an eye out for father while I'm gone," I said, feeling her smirk follow me out of the room.

The cold air in the narrow hall of our entryway, so different from the decorated foyer of our town house, served as another unpleasant reminder of how much harsher everything about this place was compared to the coast.

"Rowan." Avery Lockland's broad frame took up the doorway and blocked the dim light of the winter sky. His dark brown hair curled disobediently on his handsome head, and his full lips smiled easily and often.

Unless, of course, he was looking at me. Then he didn't smile so much as grimace.

I could feel Aspen's eyes sticking to my back like pine sap. Aspen would have smiled up at Avery with all the reserve of a mare in heat. Probably had, but that was not something I cared to think about.

"Hello, Avery." His name tasted like ash and brittle bones.

"It's a beautiful day," he said, gesturing at the sleet spitting down from the glowering sky. "Care for a walk?"

A gust of wind blew the sleet into my face. I braced myself as the ice stung my cheeks, something in my chest aching to fly away over the trees, down the sloping lowlands to the sea, away from the shadow of the mountain and the boy who was to be my husband.

I thought about slamming the door in his face, and then, unbidden, came the thought of retreating back into the house where my father's dreams lay sleeping, and spending another afternoon staring into the fire while my hands performed the menial tasks that now defined my existence.

"I would love to," I said, taking vindictive pleasure from the look of surprise on his face. I shrugged into my cloak and took the arm he offered, stepping out into the cold. We ignored each other, walking in silence down the village lane until we came to the edge of the forest. A cardinal swooped over the path, a brilliant flash of red in the gray day.

It reminded me, with the familiar stab of pain it always brought, of my mother.

She rarely spoke of her childhood, and she had gone to great lengths to remedy her provincial past. The only signs she ever gave of missing her home were the names she chose for her daughters and the hours she spent in her garden, tending the mountain rose she'd brought with her. Rowan, Aspen, and Juniper, she'd called us. Her little mountain trees, growing in the fertile soil of the lowlands.

She had named me Rowan seventeen years ago today.

"When will your father return?" Avery asked me, stooping to scoop up a ball of sleet. He heaved it at a nearby rowan tree, his timing, as always, bitterly ironic.

"I don't know." I turned my face up to the sky, letting the freezing rain slap my cheeks and sting my lips. Better rain against my lips than Avery, I thought, remembering Aspen's parting words. At least he, too, was miserable. Only the same worry that had spurred me to accept his invitation could have pried him from his family's hunting lodge, where he could be drinking a frothing horn of ale by the massive hearth with his cronies and, more than likely, accompanied by a few of the less reputable village women. I'd only been inside once, and I had a vivid recollection of the stag's head mounted above the hearth, its antlers blackened by smoke, staring at me out of empty eyes.

I did not want to share the deer's fate, cooped up with the Lockland clan, half-dressed children with the same insolent blue eyes as the man beside me tugging on my skirts and demanding to be put to the breast.

I met those eyes by accident. There was a defensive, wary look to them that vanished the moment he saw me looking.

He did not ask to marry you either, a nasty little voice in the back of my mind reminded me. Avery was as bound to his father's ambition as I was to mine, and now both of them were somewhere in the mountains, hunting for furs to ship overseas, my father's disgrace not so total that he did not still have a few contacts eager for the exotic pelts of the north, Avery's father not so immune to the allure of promised wealth that he was willing to put his son's desires before his own personal gains.

So here we were, a pact made in flesh and blood, while the foothills of the mountains hugged the village like an anxious mother, unwilling to let her offspring stray too far into the light of progress.

A sliver of unease wormed its way into my heart.

Avery knew as well as I did that the hunting trip could take more than a month, but as the days stretched past the provisions the men had packed, he had taken to blaming my father for the delay.

"When we are married," he said, hurling another sleet ball into the trees, "I will not keep you waiting."

I didn't know if it was a promise or a threat. Coming from Avery, it could have been either.

"When we are married," I said, making a sleet ball of my own to throw into the dark, wet woods, "you will not make promises you cannot keep."

Avery laughed. He had a boyish, contagious laugh that somewhat spoiled my desire to hate him. His eyes flicked toward me again, and he hesitated. I had the impression he was weighing whether or not to call a truce.

"Do you know why my family is called Lockland?" he said.

I tucked my mittens, which were now damp with sleet, under my arms and shook my head.

"It's an old story."

I stifled the scoffing sound deep in my throat before he could hear it and turned my attention back to the woods. The mountains were full of old stories, each more laden with superstition than the last, and nothing made these people happier than reciting them as frequently as possible.

"A long time ago there was a lord named Locke."

"Locke, as in Lockland?"

"Yes," he said, missing the sarcasm in my voice.

"Locke was a mighty hunter, and he ruled his clan wisely, providing for his people in the summer and fall and in the long, cold months tanning hides so flawless you could see your reflection in the leather."

"What did he do in the spring?"

Avery paused, looking momentarily confused. "Planted crops, I expect, or sharpened his spear. Do you want to hear the story or not?"

"Of course I do," I said, forcing a smile onto my face. "I'm sorry."

"One day, Locke fell in love."

I hid my eye-roll. Handsome hunters were always falling in love in his clan's stories or, perhaps more to the point, having women fall in love with them.

"The woman he loved was beautiful, but cruel. She refused him—"

"Bet he didn't take that well," I said under my breath.

"—and then killed him."

8

I almost tripped in surprise. "Killed him?"

"I told you she was cruel."

"Why would she kill him?"

"For daring to ask for her hand? For looking at her the wrong way? For breathing? Who knows. She was a queen—"

"You never said she was a queen."

"Gods, woman, are you going to let me finish the story?"

"That depends. Are you going to tell it properly?"

Avery fell into a sullen silence, and another cardinal flitted through the woods, searching for berries.

"I'm sorry," I said for the second time that day. "What happened next?"

He looked up at the mountain above us, his thoughts joining mine as we cast them into the woods where our fathers had gone.

"She was cursed, along with her court and her castle, and Locke's father claimed what was left of the kingdom and named it after his son. Oh, I almost forgot," he said, cutting me off before I could protest the story's abrupt ending. He reached into the pocket of his jacket and withdrew a small, wooden shape. "Happy birthday." He handed the carving to me. I stared at the little wolf in my palm, curled up with its tail over its nose, an old folk blessing wishing the bearer an easy winter.

"Did you make this?" I asked, disbelief coloring my voice.

"I might have," he said, shrugging.

I stroked the smooth wood, confused and at a loss for words.

I found the weight of it in my pocket oddly comforting on the walk home as the sky lowered and the sleet turned to snow. I clung to the faint, improbable hope that the charm would work, and that the worst of winter's fury would hold off until my father returned home.

"You could try to be happy," Aspen said to me when I sat down by the fire later that afternoon. Her face looked slightly apologetic, and I felt the wooden wolf brush against my leg through my skirt.

"I am," I said, meaning it for the space it took to say the words.

Of the three of us, Aspen had adapted most gracefully to our new life. The close-mindedness and homogeneity of the mountain valley did not seem to get under her skin the way it did mine, and it probably helped that people tended to like her wherever she went. She plopped down on the hearth beside me, her concern hatching into something far more dangerous.

"You should wear rouge. You look quite pretty, with your cheeks and lips all red."

"Thanks, Aspen." I made a face at Juniper, who giggled.

"If you just took a little more care with your appearance . . ." she trailed off, evidently dreaming of the boundless opportunities this would afford me. She ran her fingers through my hair, arranging it to fall around my face in an effort to soften the sharp edges.

"You've got looks enough for the both of us," I said to her, catching her hand with mine and stopping her before she got carried away and urged me to try on one of her more fashionable dresses. There had been a time when I was jealous of my younger sister. Beauty opened doors and greased wheels, smoothing the road ahead. It also had its price. People didn't really see Aspen, only her face and her hips. At least when people looked at me there were no illusions.

"And you've got the brains," Aspen said to me.

"What does that leave me?" Juniper asked, her young face full of concern.

Aspen and I exchanged a conspiratorial glance.

"The brawn," said Aspen.

"That's right. Looks like you'll have to get used to mucking out the barn and hauling all the water," I added.

Juniper, who was growing so quickly she had a hard enough time walking and talking at the same time, glowered at us. "You're both awful."

"Be a dear, Junie, and get us something to drink? It's Rowan's birthday, after all."

"Do you think father knows he's missing it?" Juniper peered out the window at the darkening sky as she spoke.

10

"Of course he does," Aspen snapped, irritation lacing her voice. It was not enough to disguise the worry lurking beneath it. The wind caught in the chimney, and the howling sounded disconcertingly like the cry of a wolf.

"Each of you, think of a gift," my father had said before he left. "When I return, I will make a trip to town to finish closing out the estate, and I would like to bring you home something special."

I did not tell him that my home was there, in the town where my mother had lived and died, and not here, in a remote mountain valley without so much as a single library.

Juniper, whose voice at least never wobbled precariously, asked for a lute. Aspen begged him for a new dress, or at least some cloth to have new ones made here.

"What, have you already read every book in the world?" Aspen had teased me when I was slow to reply.

What use were books, I didn't say aloud, if all they did was show you worlds and lives that could never be yours?

"Bring me a rose cutting, like the ones mother grew in the garden in town," I asked instead. "Just a small one. I can plant it by the well in the spring."

Not even Aspen had anything to say to that.

My father had raised his hand to my cheek, a hand that was more calloused now than I remembered it being as a child.

"You are your mother's daughter," he said to me, and none of us missed the tears that brightened his brown eyes.

I had regretted my angry thoughts. It was not my father's fault that she was gone, any more than it was his fault that the autumn before last had boiled the sea into a roiling stew of storms, smashing his ships to jagged timbers and his fortune with it.

We had lost my mother and we had lost our home, but I could bring roses back into our lives, if nothing else.

"*Mercy.*"

She tilted her head.

The word had meant something once.

Mercy was the swift knife, following the arrow.

Mercy was the rattle in the lungs after a long sickness, the smile that slipped into sleep and faded.

Mercy was death, in the mountains.

This man smelled of wet fur and blood. At least he had not soiled himself, like the other two. Beneath the smell of hides were old odors: salt, wood, spices. Smells that did not come from the mountain.

Her lips slid down over her teeth.

She moved her tongue in her mouth, remembering the feel of words, and raised her spear.

"*Please, I have three daughters. They will starve, without me. You must let me go.*"

The spear weighed nothing in her hand. Death was as light as air.

"*You asked for mercy,*" *she said. The sounds were wrong, her pronunciation off.*

"*Yes, please, I will do anything. Anything you ask.*"

He did not understand.

Death was wiser.

Three daughters.

Pain stirred.

Once, another man had had a daughter.

Her fist tightened.

Death would have been wiser then, too.

"This is mercy," she said, and the shaft of the spear thrummed with anticipation.

"Rowan, Aspen, Juniper."

Again, she paused.

"Trees," she said. "The mountain sisters."

"My daughters. Those are their names. Rowan is the oldest. Their mother died, two years ago. If you kill me, they will lose everything."

His eyes were brown. The other men's eyes had been blue.

"You should have thought about that before you crossed the boundary and hunted down my Hounds."

"I— the boundary?"

She smelled fear in his sweat, and confusion. Did he lie? She crouched before him, the spear still steady. He lay on the ground and clutched the wounds the pack had given him.

"You are not a Lockland," she said.

"No."

The wolves snarled.

She watched his blood trickle into the snow.

She thought of more words she could say.

"I will not give you mercy," she said at last.

He closed his eyes, swallowing once.

He did not beg.

She stood.

"Do not come back."

Her words were stronger now, her voice sure. He opened his eyes when he heard them, and for all that her pronunciation was correct this time, he did not understand.

"You are letting me go?"

She brought the spear to rest against his heart.

"I am letting you go. But do not mistake freedom for mercy."

The mountain would have its due.

Chapter Two

My father shivered by the fire, his eyes locked in ice while Aspen, Juniper, and I tried to coax warm broth down his throat. My hands shook as I stirred the kettle over the flames. I had been the one to see to his horse while my sisters carried him inside. Beneath the icicles, I had found deep scratches, either from claws or thorns or jagged rock, I could not be certain, but the blood had frozen with the ice, turning the familiar brown gelding into a strange blood bay. It had taken the better part of an hour for me to rub him down, and the harness had creaked like winter trees as I lifted it off his broad back.

"Where are the others?" I asked the horse, running a clean rag over him to dry the sweat that had not yet frozen. The horse leaned against me in response, blowing clouds of steam out of his bleeding nostrils.

The sledge loomed large in the darkness of the barn, death piled high atop its icy runners. I dropped the cloth in the straw. Sprawled above the others, its white fur gleaming even in the dim light, lay the largest wolf I had ever seen. It had not been skinned like the other carcasses, and its frozen, dead eyes watched me.

I stumbled out of the barn in my haste to get away from the monster. I did not want to think about my father facing such a beast, nor did I want to think about the wounds in the horse's flank, or where Avery's father and older brother had gone.

Back inside, my father thawed slowly. Juniper sponged the blood from his face and beard while Aspen held his hand. I kept the fire going and the broth hot, dreading the words that would inevitably spill like the broth from his blue lips.

"Rowan," he said at last, struggling to raise his head. "I have a gift for you."

My heart pounded in anticipation and in fear. Of all the things I had expected him to say, that was the least likely. He pointed at his coat. In the large front pocket I saw a leather packet. Frost glittered on the hide.

I opened it with my back to my sisters, unwrapping the bloody sinew that he had used to seal it shut. Inside, nestled in a bed of snow, lay a single white rose. The petals felt soft and lush beneath my finger, the delicate leaves a green so dark they looked almost black in the light of the fire. I picked it up. Snow clung to the stem, and as I turned to face my father one of the curving thorns bit into the palm of my hand. I stared at the bead of blood, red against the white.

The rose stirred. I almost dropped it in shock, and another thorn nipped at me, this time piercing my forefinger. At the base of the rose where my father's knife had severed the flower from the bush, a thin tendril of root crept out, moving like frost across my palm. It was cold against my skin, and I stared, fascinated, as the root tendrils soaked up the blood like it was water, taking root in the wound.

"Rowan?" Aspen's voice broke the spell.

I blinked, and the rose was just a rose, and I was standing in the kitchen of my father's house with ice melting down my wrist.

"Where did you find this?" I asked him, turning to face the fire.

His face looked haunted.

Aspen held out her hand to take the rose from me, curiosity alight in her eyes. My fingers closed around the stem involuntarily and I stifled a gasp of pain as the thorns bit deeper. I did not look this time to see if my hand was covered in hoarfrost. I could feel it like ice in my veins.

Aspen recoiled from the expression on my face, looking younger than her sixteen years.

"Rowan," my father said, his eyes fluttering shut. "I am so cold, Rowan."

"Wrap another blanket around him," I told my sisters, fear chilling my heart further. I wanted to ask him where he had found this flower, and I wanted to ask him what had happened to Avery's father and brother and why they had not stopped to skin the white wolf, but his cheeks were flushed with fever.

I put the rose in a vase of water on the kitchen table and helped my sisters carry my father to his bed. Aspen kept sneaking cautious looks at me out of the corner of her large, doe's eyes, and I wondered what she had seen on my face. Wondered, but did not ask, because the wounds in my palm were strangely chilled and a skin of ice had formed over the water in the vase despite the warmth of the fire.

I did not tell my sisters about the wolf.

I lay awake long into that night, fearing my dreams, but when they finally came I dreamt of spring. Meltwater ran down the mountains into our valley, washing away memories of winter, blood, and Avery Lockland. I walked through a newly green field and for the first time since my mother's death I felt light.

"Rowan." Juniper shook my shoulder. Her breath steamed in the air. I hovered in the warm green space of the dream for a moment longer.

"Father?" I asked, sitting up in a tangle of sheets as yesterday came back to me.

"Sleeping," she said in a hushed voice. Her pale face shone in the darkness. "Listen."

Wind battered the thatch. It rustled through the walls, worrying the chinks between stone and board and prying at the shutters. Behind the wind, carried down from the foothills by the blizzard's wrath, came the sound of wolves. Juniper's hand tightened on mine. "There are so many of them," she said.

17

"And a door between us." I squeezed her hand. "We will be safe." I tucked her back into bed and lit a candle, illuminating the small room where the three of us slept. Juniper's eyes closed in the comforting promise of the light, and Aspen slept on.

I was wide awake. Doors were made of wood, and wood was not as substantial as people gave it credit for. Wooden ships were supposed to separate people from the water, and look what had happened to my father's fleet.

I shoved my feet into rabbit-fur slippers and crept into the kitchen. The banked coals glowed, and the sound of the wolves was louder. My rose gleamed on the table, its stem encased in a block of ice. In the darkness, with the wolves at the door, I found it harder to erase the memory of the thorns. I took my father's sword down from the mantle and sat by the coals with the blade across my knees while my candle cast its feeble glow over the once familiar shadows of the room.

It was not a comfortable position to fall asleep in. I woke with a crick in my neck and soot in my mouth, clutching the sword like a child with a doll. Real sunlight glowed against the curtains, and for a moment I had no idea where I was or what I was doing.

The horse.

I wiped the drool from my chin and my hand came away black with ash from where my cheek had rested. There had been wolves, and that meant that I had to check on the horse, because barn doors were also made of wood.

I hesitated, then decided to keep the sword with me, however foolish it might look to my sisters when they woke. I rebuilt the fire, grabbed the water bucket, and shrugged into my winter clothing.

Several feet of snow fell inward as I opened the door. I swore under my breath and kicked the worst of it back out, then shut the traitorous door behind me and turned to face the yard.

The sun was a pink stain on the horizon, and the edges of the forest were still soft and gray. Everything else was white. The barn was blasted with snow, and the well was a vague lump in the center of the yard. I put one foot in front of the other and forced my way

18

through the drifts to the big barn doors. They were still shut, which seemed promising, and the dread lifted its hold on me until I remembered the dead wolf on the other side. I gripped the cold hilt of the sword, shouldered open the door, and slipped into the musty darkness.

It smelled like hay and living, breathing horse. I scooped some grain into his bucket and broke the ice on the trough, forking some more hay into the rack. Satisfied that all was well, I allowed myself to run past the sledge without looking and escape back into the morning.

A white shape moved against the trees.

The sword hung heavy in my hands, and my mouth dried as the wolf stared back at me. I thought about ducking back into the barn, but if my sisters found me missing they would come looking for me and then this wolf might go after them instead, not that wolves often attacked humans, but—the wolf turned tail and loped away, leaving me alone with my racing thoughts.

I waited for several long minutes before making my way to the well. Scraping the snow off the lid required that I take my attention away from the tree line, which sent the hairs on the back of my neck into a state of intense alarm. I hauled the water up so quickly that half of it spilled, and I had to lower it again, this time taking long, deep breaths to still my shaking hands.

The wolf did not return. I cast anxious glances back over my shoulder as I struggled to balance sword and bucket while also navigating thigh-deep drifts. It was in one such backward glance that I saw them. A few yards from the door, perfect and clear in the lightening yard, was a set of prints that did not belong to a wolf. I set the bucket down and edged closer.

The print was larger than my hand, larger than three of my hands, with long, dark gouges in the snow from impossibly long claws. I stared at the bear prints and felt my heart freeze over. No door could have withstood an assault from paws that size. Not the door to our house, not the door to the barn, and not even the door to the city gates that had closed shut behind me, forever altering the course of my life.

The tracks circled the yard, obscured here and there by a drift before retreating back into the forest. "Father," I whispered into the cold, clear air. "What have you brought with you?"

My father slept most of the day, his skin hot to the touch and his eyes fevered. When we removed his clothes, we discovered three long gashes on his thigh that glared angrily out of his puckered flesh.

I didn't mention the bear prints to my sisters, and I didn't dare draw comparisons between the wounds on his leg and the claws in the snow. The wolf had been alarming enough. Instead, I ground herbs into a poultice and prepared more broth, taking a mental inventory of our larder and cursing the forebearer who had built the house out of sight of the village. I was not walking down that wooded lane.

The wolves returned that night. I lay awake long after my sisters' ragged breathing subsided into the calm, measured breaths of sleep, listening to the mournful howls and the sound of my father coughing.

Tomorrow I would have to go in search of the village herbalist, and someone had to find Avery to discover whether his father and brother had returned by a different route. I had contrived to keep my sisters in the house for today, which was easy enough, given my father's health and the bitter cold that had descended, and I had taken a broom to the prints near the door as if erasing them would erase their maker.

Tomorrow, the frozen bubble that had enveloped our house would burst, thrusting us back into the world.

Frost spread outward from the vase on the table, and the rose opened a new bud, the faintest pink visible in its veins. I gave it a wide berth. I was beginning to think there was something very wrong with that rose.

I must have drifted into sleep sometime after midnight, because the night was old when the scratching started. It roused me from a dream of warm rain and melting snow, a horrible, wrenching sound of shrieking wood and deep animal breathing. Something was clawing at the door.

I sat bolt upright and met two more pairs of terrified eyes.

"What the hell is that?" asked Aspen.

"I don't know," I said, because I didn't know, not really. A bear scratching at the door was just as likely as a bull moose, or a madman, or a dragon. Well, maybe not a dragon. These things didn't happen, not in town, and not even in quiet upland villages.

"What do we do?" asked Juniper.

"Stay here," I told them, slipping my feet once again into the soft down of my slippers and padding into the kitchen to take the sword down from the mantel. Out here, I could hear the snuffling of some wintry creature working its nose along the cracks of the door. I ran back into our bedroom with the sword held tightly in both hands and bolted the door, then shoved the dresser we shared in front of it.

"What about father?"

"He will be fine, and he would want us to protect ourselves," I said, ashamed of my fear. I should have led us all to his room and barred that door. I should not have given in to the suspicion that the bear was after him, a dark, cold, slimy thought that was not quite as brave as the blade I laid again across my knees, preparing for another vigil.

I could not prevent my sisters from peering out the door the next morning. We stood, three dark heads against the white of the fresh snow, staring at the long, pale gouges something had scratched into the red wood of our front door. Something, and not someone. No tool could make those marks, and no man had left those tracks.

In the smallest of blessings, my father's fever broke that morning, sparing us the need to go for the herbalist. We moved him back to the kitchen onto a pallet by the fire, and Juniper sang to him while I cooked and Aspen stoked the flames. Every now and then I would go to the door, expecting to see pale golden eyes watching me from the forest. All I saw was the occasional flash of wings as the birds searched for food amid the drifts.

Mercy.

She remembered so many things now.

To spare a life was to ensure suffering.

Death was surer.

He would learn that.

She knelt by his tracks, resting her hand against the deep print of his boots.

Mercy.

He should never have touched the roses.

She stared at the briars. His tracks led past them, winding down the mountain to the soft green lands beyond, death somewhere on his person.

One step, and she was past the thorns.

Two steps, and she was free, free for as long as the rose stayed in his hands.

Thief.

She growled deep in her throat.

She should have killed him. Instead, she would show him the meaning of loss, as it had been shown to her.

Her howl swept down the mountain like the fall of a knife, sowing fear in its wake.

As he had taken, so would she.

As she had lost, so would he.

A rose for a rose, a thorn for a thorn.

Chapter Three

He called us to him as the daylight waned.

"My daughters," he said, his voice a low rasp. "I was afraid I would never see you again."

We waited for more.

"I am so very, very sorry for all of the trouble I have brought on you."

Aspen assured him that he had brought no trouble at all. Juniper stroked his hand. I met his eyes. There was terror in their depths, and a regret that surpassed the loss of friends and business.

"I am so very, very sorry." Tears rolled down his cheeks.

"Father," I said, earning shocked looks from my sisters for my tone. "What happened? Where are the Locklands?"

"Rowan." Aspen shook her head at me. "He is ill. He needs rest, not questions."

"Please, Rowan," said Juniper, her lower lip quivering.

I looked into their faces. Neither of them had stopped to consider what would happen to us if Avery's father and brother were dead. The reasons for our flight from the city were well known, and in the mountains, where superstition held sway over logic and curses exacted justice, I did not want to think about what our neighbors would decide to do with us between now and the spring thaw, should they conclude we had brought our bad luck with us.

"She is right to ask," my father said to them, sitting up with

24

painful slowness and placing a wind-roughened hand on his injured leg. "I should have stayed in the mountains." He hushed my sisters' protests. "I must speak to Avery."

"Tomorrow," I said, thinking of the beasts outside the door. "Aspen's right. You need rest." I paused, no longer sure if I wanted answers. "Are they . . .?"

"Dead," he said. In the silence that followed his words, he murmured something else.

"What did he say?" I asked my sisters.

"'Mercy,'" said Aspen, turning to me in confusion. "He said 'mercy.'"

"Mercy brought you home," I told him.

He made a strangled sound, and it took me a few seconds to realize it was laughter. Then his eyes focused, and he saw the sword leaning against the hearthstone.

It had been a terrible thing to see my father cry, and more terrible still to see him afraid, but nothing was as terrible as the sight of despair breaking him, aging him, crippling him before my eyes.

Outside, the wind picked up. My sisters huddled closer together, and all four of us stared at the door. My gaze faltered on the rose. The entire table had frosted over in a sheet of ice, and the rose looked fuller, more alive than any cut flower had a right to be.

"Where did you get that rose?" I asked.

My father didn't answer. The howling started again, closer this time than ever before, and something large and primal roared outside the door.

The beast did not use its claws this time. Instead, I heard the distinctive crunch of booted human feet landing on the doorstep, and the unmistakable sound of a human fist knocking, once, twice, three times on the wooden door.

"Get behind me," my father said, straightening his now hunched back and brandishing the sword before him.

The stranger knocked again. Once, twice, thrice.

"Who is it?" Aspen asked in a shaky whisper.

I felt ice stir in my veins.

I remembered the prick of thorns in my palm.

I watched as the door burst open, shattered by a great white paw as the head and shoulders of an ice bear burst through the doorway, bellowed once, then retreated.

I heard the slow step of feet picking their way through shattered timbers, and a brutal gust of wind whipped snow into the room in frenzied flurries.

"Stay back," my father shouted, and I loved him for his bravery even as I knew that there was nothing he could do to protect us against what was coming.

A tall figure emerged through the snow, dressed in a long, white fur cloak with a hood that shadowed its face. My hand tingled, the way fingers and toes do when they have been exposed to cold for far too long.

The figure raised gloved hands and lowered its hood.

My father trembled. Aspen screamed. Juniper staggered and clutched at my sleeve to keep from falling.

I stared.

I had been wrong to think that the colors of winter were merely silver and white, I found myself thinking. There was the black of wet tree bark; the bruised blue of shadowed drift; the deep, undimmed green of the pines; and the harsh shock of red blood across snow.

The woman standing in our kitchen was all of these and more.

Red lips curled in a mocking smile. Dark green eyes challenged my father from a face pale with the first flush of a winter sunset, framed with hair the brown of the last of autumn's leaves beneath the snow, the darkness limning distant trees, and the blue-black fall of a winter night.

"Where is it," the woman said. It was not a question. She examined each of us in turn, and when her eyes fell on me at last, a thrill went through me.

"Where is what?" I asked, my words little more than a whisper.

"My rose."

I pointed.

She was at the table in a single stride, plucking the rose out from the ice as easily as if it had been water. Maybe it was water. Maybe the ice was in my eyes, or in my veins, and the rose was just a rose and none of this was happening.

"A rose for a rose, a thorn for a thorn." When none of us spoke or asked for clarification, she took a step toward me. "You," she said, and her voice, at least, was human.

"*No.*" The word ripped from my father's throat with such violence that I thought I might see blood on his lips.

"These are your daughters?" the woman asked. When my father did not respond, she took a step closer. "When you trespassed on my land, hunting down my kin, I greeted you with more courtesy than you deserved. Put down your sword, old man."

The blade fell from my father's hands, whether of his own free will or by the force of her suggestion.

"Please, take me instead," he begged, falling to his knees in supplication.

"You took a rose from my garden. Now I shall take one from yours." Her eyes found mine again. "You must be Rowan."

Aspen understood the woman's meaning before I did. She flung herself in front of me, shielding me with her slender frame.

"Aspen," I said, ice gripping my stomach.

"You can't take her." Aspen planted her feet firmly on the hard-packed earth.

"I can, child, and I will." The bear roared again from beyond the door. "Consider yourselves lucky that I am content with just the one."

"Why?" Aspen, who I had always thought a little too conceited for her own good, rose to my defense again, finding words while the rest of us were struck dumb. "Rowan didn't do anything wrong."

"You gave her the rose?" the stranger asked my father.

"Yes," he said.

I heard his heart breaking. It echoed sounds I had only ever half imagined, the sharp crack of frozen sap, the groan of the ice floes breaking up in the spring, and the long, slow howl of the lone wolf.

"Then it is done."

My father picked up his discarded sword and charged. She knocked him to the ground with predatory ease, plucking the sword from his limp hands.

"Come with me," she said, and her words slid into my bloodstream with the scent of roses.

"Rowan, no!" Aspen grabbed my arm, and Juniper clung to my other side, sobbing.

"I spared your father's life once. I will not spare it a second time," the woman said. She raised the sword, and I pushed past my sisters to stand before her, placing my hands on the sharp edge of the blade.

"Please," I said.

Green eyes bored into mine. "From you," she said, lowering the sword, "that word sounds much sweeter." I shivered at the cold from the open door, my teeth chattering as a strange numbness filled me.

My father groaned and stirred on the floor. "Rowan," he whispered as the woman cast one last glance around the room.

"You wandered too far north, old man," she said. "Out here Winter still has teeth." She pulled me behind her, and I stepped out into the storm.

The blank security of shock abandoned me the minute I left the house. Waiting, its fur lit by the stray light of the moon, was the bear. I had seen a bear, once, from a distance. That bear had been small and black and comfortingly far away. This bear towered head and shoulders over me, its muzzle tipped with black and full of gleaming teeth. It shook its ruff and snorted, a deep, coughing sound that sent me scrabbling backward against the woman. She brushed me aside and laid a hand on the bear's snout. It snarled once, then settled, turning bright, black eyes on me.

"Come here."

I glanced around the yard, wondering how far I could make it before the bear ran me down. At the edge of the trees, a chorus of howls rose up in warning. The shaking that threatened to loosen my teeth spread to the rest of my body as the scent of the massive predator saturated my senses, and then the woman was in front of me, her eyes as black as the bear's in the darkness. She lifted me, and I was too shocked to fight her, stunned into the same terror that leaves the rabbit trembling before the fox. She swung me over the bear's broad back and I lay face down in the musky fur, my heart threatening to burst in my tight chest. Behind me, I felt the woman swing herself up. Her thigh pressed against my cheek.

I clung to it, because it was human and warm, and I prayed to all the gods I knew that she, at least, would not attempt to eat me.

"Sit," she said.

My panicked mind refused to process her words, and I clung tighter to her leg. Strong hands pried me off, and I stiffened, terror turning me into the wood of my namesake.

"Sit," she ordered again. Her voice was low and steady, the kind of voice you would use to calm a frantic animal that you were not above beating into submission if all else failed.

It worked.

She helped me straddle the beast. I felt the thick muscles of its shoulders bunching beneath me as it adjusted to the new weight and a sound escaped from the back of my throat that might have been a moan of terror, a whimper, or just my last desperate shred of sanity taking flight.

This was past understanding, past reason, and certainly past the limits of my imagination. My mind, presented with things beyond its ability to comprehend, shut down, leaving me with a pair of eyes and a frozen tongue and nothing even remotely resembling thought.

The woman wrapped a firm arm around my waist to keep me upright, bringing the heavy pelt of her cloak with her. The weight of it blocked the wind, and behind me her body was warm. I took comfort in that, because there was no other comfort to be had as the bear lumbered out of the yard I had once hated for its strangeness, and now had never loved more.

The girl slumped against her, and unbidden she remembered the boy.

A man, he had called himself, striding into her hall with his father's colors gleaming on his chest, but a boy for all his brave words, and as green as summer. Three times, Locke had pressed his suit, his eyes barely able to meet hers, and three times she had refused him, laughing with her Hounds as he backed out of her presence.

"I love you," he told her the last time. "Let me prove it to you."

She had turned away, bored by the game, but her Hounds had stopped her.

"Let him," Brendan had said, his big hands resting on the long muzzle of his wolfhound. "Let us see what he is made of."

"Go," she'd told Locke, ignoring Brendan. "Go, run home to your lord father and tell him I will have you when this mountain turns to ash and the lakes boil. Or, perhaps, I will have your sister. Is she as pretty as you?"

Locke had stammered out something incoherent, and Quince moved restlessly, hair like blown leaves shadowing her narrow face. "It is past time we had a decent hunt. I'm bored with winter. Let him hunt with us."

She had paused then, surprised by Quince's words.

She fell into the memory, the smell of spring as sharp as glass, as warm and clean as the soft smell of the girl's hair.

"Please. Let me prove myself worthy," Locke had said, ever eager.

"There is nothing to hunt," she said, turning, once again, to leave the boy behind.

"There is always bear." Quince tossed the words, light as air, but

brittle. She looked at Quince then, and saw something far more interesting than the lordling's pleas.

"Even a lean bear would feed his father's entourage," said Brendan, his deep voice rumbling through the hall. "Let him hunt with us and earn his place here, instead of feasting on better hunters' kills."

"Spring bear is dangerous," she told Locke. "They wake up angry. Miss a throw, and you're dead."

"I would do anything for you."

It was his earnestness that repelled her. It was too much, coming from his handsome face—like a picture, or a poem. Still, she could tell something about him had gotten under Quince's skin. She touched her Hound's shoulder, and Quince dropped those quick, dark eyes.

Her blood stirred. There was game to be had, here, somewhere.

"Then let us ride."

She remembered the taste of melting snow. It had dripped from the trees, darkening her horse's mane and staining her breeches. Meltwater ran in rills and rivulets, stirring the dark, damp scents of soil and new growth.

Locke rode a blood-red mountain bay. His blue eyes watched her, his full lips determined. Poets sang about such boys, she thought, spurring her mare forward. There were no poets, here.

The dogs found the bear as the spring sun set the trees alight, gold spinning webs around the red and green buds. On his hind legs, the bear stood taller than two men, and winter had not wasted the muscle on his enormous frame.

"Call off the dogs," said Brendan, his voice as close to her now as it had felt far off then.

Call them off, *she willed the past, but the wish did not change history this time, either.*

"No," she'd said instead, and she remembered the feel of that cold smile. "Locke, I swear upon my life that if you bring me that bear's heart I will be yours until my dying breath."

Quince's horse shifted, and the look that passed between them burned her through the years, wasted, useless, a mockery of feeling.

Of course he died.

Of course he charged, his horse's eyes wild with fear as he raised his spear and sent it toward the beast.

His aim was true, but his arm too weak, or else the bear too strong. The claws ripped him nearly in half, and it had taken all of them to bring the creature down. Three dogs died, too, and she had pressed her fingers to their quivering flanks, their lives fluttering beneath her fingers. Her favorite licked her hand, then shuddered, and she forgot about Locke until Quince laughed.

"Look," Quince had said, and she had.

The boy lay with his dark hair soaked in blood and his blue eyes wide with shock. His breathing came in fits, and she stood over him, her shadow blocking the sunlight from his eyes.

He said her name and fumbled in the pocket of his jacket with clumsy fingers.

"He brought you a rose," Quince said, still laughing.

"Perhaps," she had said, kneeling beside Locke and lifting the flower from his trembling fingers, "he should have brought a second spear instead."

Chapter Four

My family's screams followed us into the snow. I looked back as best I could as the bear began to move, struggling against the woman's grip as the slow lumber gathered speed like an avalanche. I saw my father sprawled in a drift, one arm outstretched towards me, my name on his lips as he shouted himself hoarse. He must have tried to run and fallen, his wounded leg giving out beneath him before he could make it to the clearing's edge. Aspen had Juniper wrapped in her arms, keeping them both upright as they swayed with horror, and Juniper's sobs echoed in my ears long after the trees obscured my vision and my family faded from sight, lost to me in the gloaming.

That night stretched into a cold morning. I woke at one point, shivering, to find that I had turned against her, my head lolling on her shoulder. I ached with cold and exhaustion and fear, and a new stiffness. Riding a giant bear was nothing like riding a horse, and I had never ridden a horse through the night. My thighs ached. My rear ached. My heart ached, and I wondered what my sisters and father were doing now, as daylight brought the reality of the night into harsh clarity. I wondered if I would ever see any of them again.

We rode through dark forests full of pine and fir and black out-croppings of rock, slick with ice and shadow. Ahead and behind ranged the wolves. I counted seven in number, though it was hard to tell them apart. The only one I was sure I hadn't counted twice was as black as the rocks we passed.

The bear lumbered through the drifts, a tireless pace that jarred me to my frozen core. Elk scattered in the higher clearings, snorting plumes of steam and shaking their great antlers. From a distance, I thought I saw the swift fall of a mountain lion descending on something small and white, although it could have been nothing more than a gust of windblown snow.

The air grew thinner the higher we climbed, catching in my throat and burning in my lungs. My captor pressed on, keeping a pace that would have killed a man on horseback, or even a man on a dogsled. Nothing natural moved the way her beasts did, and the wind from our passage creaked through the trees.

We came at last to a vast frozen lake high amid the peaks. The bear paused on the shore, and across the ice rose the highest point in the spine of my world, a peak so tall that the clouds felt miles below us. At the base of that peak, overlooking the lake, was a keep. The wolves yipped, setting out toward it at a steady lope, and the bear coughed deep in its chest. The roots that the rose had put deep in my flesh stirred again.

Home.

The lake itself was at least a mile across, maybe more. The wind stirred the snow on its surface, which swirled and danced and fell apart, small whirlwinds obscuring the castle from view. By the time we passed beneath the shadow of that mountain, the sun was setting once again, staining the walls of the keep a deep pink. The castle hugged the mountain, and three towers erupted from behind the battlements. The central tower rose above the others, marching up the side of the mountain like an absurd chimney. At the very top, a candle flickered.

It was only as we passed through the huge iron gate that I noticed the roses. They grew in abundance along the lakeshore and covered the stones like enchanted ivy. A sob clawed at my chest.

The woman helped me down off the bear. My legs collapsed

as they hit the ground, weak and useless. Snow spilled into my collar, chill against my breast, and I gazed up at the bear looming like a mountain above me.

"You must be hungry," she said.

It took me several long moments to determine whether she was talking to me or the bear. My eyes traveled reluctantly away from the shaggy flanks to her face. No flicker of expression betrayed the emotions behind her mask of ice. Green eyes. Dark hair. Red lips. Her features burned like cold iron, and I flinched away from them.

How could I be hungry? How could I think of food when my legs were numb with cold and I was as far away from home as it was possible to be?

My stomach grumbled.

The snow bit deeper into my knees.

The stranger extended a gloved hand and I took it, wobbling as my legs remembered their duty.

She led me through a darkened stable that smelled of wolf, bear, and wild things my nose could not identify, a heady, animal musk that sent my muscles into new spasms of terror. Heavy stone arches and broad timbers delineated the stalls, and the wood bore the dark stains of centuries. A few long hairs clung to the roughened doors, the only evidence that horses had once dwelt there. At the end of the stable stood another stone archway, large enough to accommodate a rider on horseback. The door swung open on greased hinges at her touch.

Three of the wolves accompanied us; the rest remained in the stable, where I heard the distinctive sounds of carnivores ripping into flesh. I was glad of the darkness. I did not want to know what her creatures fed on. The woman lit a torch from a sconce and went on. The sound of the striking flint echoed, emphasizing the cavernous feel of the place, and shadows danced on the walls, throwing the rangy silhouettes of the wolves into sharp relief.

The hallway beyond the stable opened into a great hall, empty now, with sagging tables shoved against the far wall and the dais cleared of all furniture entirely. Tapestries moldered, flickering in the torchlight. The remaining rags depicted hunting scenes: muscular horses charging bristling boars, slashed through here and there by disturbingly large claw marks. I stayed close to the woman, even as a small voice warned me that her humanity was a trap. If this castle was the lair of a beast, there was only one candidate for its queen. Her dark hair shifted in the light, more like shadow than anything cast by the torch.

The deserted hall led eventually to a low flight of stairs, bringing with it warmer air as the steps curved around a pillar that looked as if it had been hewn from the mountain itself. The wolves jostled against me, their fur brushing my cold fingers, their paws silent on the stone, and then we were in the kitchen. Here, herbs hung in fragrant bunches from the rafters, and a long, low fireplace radiated warmth from its banked coals. A heavy iron kettle hung over it and the rich smell of meat stew overwhelmed me.

"Sit," she said, pointing to a worn but clean table. Its surface was an unbroken slab of wood, milled from a tree that must have towered over its neighbors in height and girth. She tossed her bearskin cloak over the far end of the table and stooped to stoke the flames while the wolves settled down around the hearth, panting past gleaming teeth and hot red tongues. One turned and licked at its hind leg. Pink blood stained the white fur. She scolded it in a soft voice, and the leather of her jerkin gleamed in the rising flames. I watched the light shift over it, making shapes and faces that I half recognized. I jumped when she straightened, the trance broken.

She placed a bowl of stew on the table, full of venison, potatoes, carrots, turnips, onions and greens, and seasoned with fresh herbs. The rising steam wreathed my face and thawed my lips and nose. My stomach grumbled again.

You may as well eat, said a timid voice in the back of my mind. Reason, it seemed, had decided to reappear, this time on the side of my traitorous stomach. I picked up the wooden spoon and took a bite. I had not had anything to eat since I left my father's house, and my insides roared to life at the taste of food.

Warmth followed the meal. It crawled back into my limbs on silent paws, leaving faint impressions on my skin.

So did her gaze.

She watched me eat, her green eyes glowing like the wolves', until I wiped my chin with my sleeve self-consciously and tucked my knees up to my chest. She ate her own stew more slowly, giving me time to observe her, although I did not dare look at her face. Gold threads shot through the thick, black wool of her sleeves and the heavy northern collar laced around her throat. I followed the leather thong up her throat, but that was too close to her face for comfort. I resumed my contemplation of her sleeves.

It was good wool. Coarse and heavy, but spun with a softer fleece to offer warmth and comfort. Beneath it, I told myself, would be a lighter tunic, also wool, spun from mountain sheep and dyed with walnuts. Hunting clothes: warm, practical, human.

She stood, affording me a glimpse of her belt. Several pouches, a flask, a long knife and a short knife, and a curved horn with a silver rim hung over her right hip. Hunting accoutrements. Leather breeches over wool leggings to fend off the cold. Scratches in the leather, dark stains around the knees from use. She wiped her knife on her left thigh after sharpening, the way Avery did. I could tell from the sheen the oilstone left on the leather.

"Here."

She walked like a wolf, light on her feet and alert but confident in her supremacy as she seized a flagon from a shelf and poured a stream of dark red wine into two drinking horns. I picked up the closest one and brought it to my lips.

She did not acknowledge my gasp of surprise, and so I drank deeply, aware that this was the sort of wine my father had reserved for the wealthiest of his clients, back when he still had clients to appease. It was strong, barely watered, and it flushed the cold from underneath my skin. I drank, and as I drank I gathered my courage the way young girls gather fleece from hedgerows and stone walls for their spindles. It felt just as wispy.

"Who are you?" I asked.

She smiled at me. It was a wolf's smile, full of teeth. "They call me the Huntress."

The name stirred a memory of some old folk tale told over a winter's evening. I must have heard it in the mountains, for it was not a tale I remembered hearing in my coastal town where the winters were mild. I frowned, unable to bring the memory closer. *You laughed at their superstitions,* I thought. *Now look at you.*

"Is that your real name?" I asked. The effort of speaking left me winded, and I tried to breathe slowly.

"It is as real a name as any."

She took a drink, sitting on a stool by the fire, her long legs stretched out in front of her while the flames licked life into the dark leather of her boots. She was beautiful in the way that a blizzard is beautiful. It hurt my chest to look at her, and I knew if I gazed for too long frostbite would work its way into my extremities and the air would freeze in my throat.

"I'm Rowan," I said. Maybe if I gave her my name, she would not feed me to the wolves.

"I know."

I didn't have any more questions after that. My bowl of stew was empty, and the table looked as likely a place to lay my head as any. I was dimly aware that she guided me to my feet, leading me up another flight of stairs and into a room with a bed and a fire. I tumbled into the bed and fell asleep before I had finished pulling the furs over me.

She paced. *The motion was as natural to her as breathing, her boots brushing the stone as lightly as the pads of the wolf beside her. Snow spilled out around them, wreathed in freezing fog. Snow, ice, thorn. That was her world. Those were the boundaries. Those were her boundaries.*

She growled, turning on her heel in frustration as she approached the end of the battlement.

Damn that man. Damn him and his reaching hands and damn her for her pity. She should have killed him. She should have ripped his throat out, as he and his hunters had done to two of her Hounds, painting the snow red and calling down the ravens to pluck out his sad brown eyes.

The girl had his eyes.

A rose for a rose, a thorn for a thorn.

She turned again, her gloved fingertips brushing the fur of the wolf beside her, and pulled the rose the man had stolen from her breast pocket to stare at the crushed petals.

White. No hint of red. Her Hounds had found it in time.

She looked closer.

Did the palest hint of pink run through its veins?

She held it up, letting the full light of the moon fall over it.

No.

Fog kissed her cheek, curling her hair into ringlets of ice. For a moment, she had doubted. She closed her eyes. Memory pounced from beneath her lids, riding fear to the surface.

"Rose for a rose, thorn for a thorn,
That is the price of true love scorned."

The witch had spoken with a voice chipped from the flint hills, laden with the promise of summer and heavy with snow.

"What do you want, old woman?" the Huntress had asked.

Her Hounds had quieted, and even the dogs stopped whining. Only the boy's ragged breathing broke the stillness, and then that, too, was gone.

The witch watched out of eyes that reflected only sky and smiled, her nut-brown face as seamed as old bark and just as yielding.

"Do you toss away true love so lightly, Isolde?"

The Huntress's hand tightened on the rose. She gasped as the thorns pierced her, in surprise more than pain, and a drop of her blood fell on the boy's torn chest. The witch smiled.

"True love? He was a child," said the Huntress.

The woman leaned on her stick, still smiling.

"A child willing to die for you."

"That is not love. That is idiocy."

"And yet you bleed." The witch stepped closer, holding out her hand to take the Huntress's.

"Roses," the Huntress spat, tossing the flower aside and shaking off the old woman.

"You would scorn them, too?"

There was a storm brewing in the question. She had felt it even then, but had not heeded it.

"I have no use for roses."

"No use for love, and no use for roses. Tell me, Isolde, what do you have a use for?" The witch raised a finger stained with a single drop of blood to her lips as she spoke.

"This." The Huntress opened her arms, gesturing to the forest and shoving fear aside. "The hunt. My Hounds. Not roses, not the love of some pup, and certainly not you."

"Ah."

The hair on the back of her neck prickled, as it did before thunder broke over the mountains. When the witch spoke next, she had heard each word as a crack of lightning.

"For your pride, you may keep your castle and your forests, but only beasts will roam your halls, and all those you love will turn to tooth and claw and cloven hoof, save you. *You shall be just as you are, colder than a winter star and just as lovely, and you shall live among them, a huntress, a queen among the bones, until the day comes when you learn what it is like to love helplessly, hopelessly, and truly. Only then will you be free, but freedom will bring you no joy, because the price of freedom will be the loss of one you cannot bear to lose.*

"Until then, I will bind you and yours with ice and thorn, until the years have stripped the memory of warmth from your bones and the only thing that blooms within your kingdom is the winter rose. As long as those roses grow wild, you shall reign over winter and all her beasts, but beware: where the winter rose takes root, it grows, and its blossoming will mark the end of everything that you now hold dear."

The Huntress forced her eyes open, but the witch's words still echoed off the moon-drenched mountains.

It did not matter.

The rose, idly plucked, had not rooted.

Chapter Five

I woke in a room with a curving outer wall and a feel of old wealth clinging to the stones. The fire had burned low during the night, and the chill forced me out from under the furs to add some wood from the stack beside the grate. In its smoky light, I saw old tapestries shot through with silver and gold threads, the colors muted with age and the tapestries' occupants faceless and faded. A heavy curtain hung over the only window. I dragged a few of the larger furs off the bed and wrapped myself in them, pausing to stroke the velvet of the drapes before I exposed a forearm to the cold and unlatched the shutter.

Snow and mountain after mountain spilled out before me, the entire eastern range marching away into the sunrise like the craggy backs of grazing cattle. Below, the frozen lake shone like a polished mirror in the brightness of the sun, the snow blinding. Clouds floated past the window, or maybe it was freezing fog; this high up it was hard to tell. Somewhere down there lay the valley where my father and sisters and I had lived, and beyond the mountains, out of sight, lay the sea.

Somewhere, but so far beyond my reach it might as well have been the moon.

Wind gusted past the window and into the room. It cut through the furs, stripping away the warmth that still clung to my sleep-soft skin. It took several breaths before I realized the rattling sound in my ears was not the shutter, but my teeth.

All that snow. All that ice. There was no way on this once-green earth that I could find my way home, even if I managed to escape. I shut the window slowly, the dark wood eclipsing the harsh light, and with it, hope.

Time passed.

I did not check the progress of the wintry sun, but the wood burned in the grate and I added more, staring at the flames until they flickered, low and blue, and I was forced to move my hand to fetch another log. Rough pine, burning hot, and the occasional hardwood. If I had been raised in the mountains, I would have known their names. If I had been raised in the mountains, I might have stood a chance.

A knock on the door set my heart to pounding. I stared at the thick, wooden boards. There was no lock from the inside. All she had to do was open it, and she would find me huddled on the rug by the fire, unarmed, my face streaked with ash and tears.

Silence stretched.

I heard the soft clatter of wood on stone, and then nothing. She walked so quietly that it was impossible to tell if she had left, or if she stood, as poised as a mountain lion, waiting.

The fire died again, and my mind slipped away, sliding down the mountains to the hard-packed dirt road that led to the gray gates of the city.

I had seen the gates only a few times. We had no cause to leave the city, at least not by land. Sometimes my father took us out in a little boat, rowed by the bear of a man he kept with us for such outings. Henrik was his name. He had a long, blond mustache that Aspen liked to tug. We didn't see that many blond men in the city, but not many people stared at Henrik for long, with his scarred face and his massive fists, imposing in their strength when wrapped around the oars, but gentle enough when he lifted us one by one onto the docks.

The Ice Bear, my mother had called him.

My thoughts skidded away, fleeing those crowded wharfs and the bright skirts I'd worn and taking shelter in the stables where my father kept his horses. A big red roan for riding, and a matched team of blacks for the carriage, stabled side by side in the wide, clean barn that smelled of hay and the occasional salt breeze from the ocean. My mother's horse flickered in and out of memory, golden, with a mane as white as snow.

No.

Father had sold that horse when she took sick, to help pay for the doctors and later the magicians and finally the funeral. Sara had held me as they led my mother's horse away. Sara, whose quick laugh and quicker hands taught me how to mend and clean the black leather harness and braid the black ribbons into the team's tails. Sara, who had found the brown gelding and the cart for us when no one else had dared touch my father's ruinous debts.

"For you," she'd said to me, pulling me out of sight. "Get the hell out of here, Rowan."

And then she'd kissed me, full on the lips, her dark eyes searching mine. Whatever she saw made her grin; a twist of her laughing mouth, the familiar tilt of her head, the sweet smells of hay and grain and horse clinging to her rough-spun tunic.

If I could only get a message to her now.

Sara, I would write, *I need another horse, another cart, another traveling cloak to shield my face, only this time it's not the banks I'm running from, but . . .*

My mind skipped again, and I found myself in the garden of our town house, the walls built with smooth stones and covered in climbing roses. They had reminded my mother of home.

I stood, the furs falling to the floor and my chest heaving. There were no roses in my mother's village. None that I had seen, at least.

The wild hope died at once. If my mother had ever been here, to this strange castle, she would have told us, or at least my father. She would not have left us without some sort of warning, nor would she have doted on those roses. Pinks and reds, never whites, I remembered, now. I never saw a white rose in her garden. Not like the ones that bloomed here.

The rush of feeling faded, but it had banished the lethargy that had borne me through the morning, and I crossed the floor to the door, listening with my ear pressed hard against the crack. When I was sure that nothing breathed beyond, I opened it. A tray lay just outside. I glanced around, but nothing stirred in the hallway. My stomach grumbled as I took a cursory inventory. Bread, and another bowl of stew with the fat congealing on the surface. A pitcher of water and a small tin cup. Food fit for a prisoner.

After eating, I tried to drift back into the warm place between despair and nothingness where memory came and went like waves, but the food had roused me. It was good bread, full of the taste of summer. I fingered the crust. Wheat did not grow on this mountain, nor did the Huntress strike me as the sort of woman who would willingly mill her own flour, which could mean only one thing: the bread came from elsewhere, and any contact with the outside world was an opportunity I could snatch if I kept my wits about me.

I soaked up the cool stew with the heel of the bread and took a closer look at the room. The first thing I noticed was the lack of dust. I had spent the last year shouldering the burden of the departed housekeeper, and I knew what it took to keep a large house clean. A few cobwebs hung in the highest corners, but the drapes on the bed looked clean, if faded, and the floor was smooth and free of debris.

Maybe the Huntress had an army of servants at her command, I thought, hope rising in me again. Human servants, instead of beasts. A human could be coerced into compassion.

My eyes scanned the room for further proof of human hands. The floor bore no marks of broom or mop that I could see, but good servants left no evidence of their passage.

At the foot of the bed I found a chest. I ran my hand over the curved top, thinking of chests full of silk sinking to the bottom of the sea. The metal bindings were cold to the touch, but the latch lifted easily, revealing neatly folded clothes and the smells of lanolin and old perfume.

I hesitated before touching them, suddenly afraid. The room echoed with half-heard voices, the former occupant watching me from the shadows behind the drapes.

Don't be an idiot, I told myself. *You have much larger things to fear than ghosts.*

I lifted the first garment from the chest. A lambswool long-sleeved tunic, dyed hunter green. Warm. I set it aside. Chamois leggings; leather breeches; soft, wool undershirts; and thick stockings. A winter wardrobe, and at the bottom, beneath the sweaters and the folded cloak, two dresses.

I pulled them out, Aspen's voice in my head as the wool ran through my fingers. The first was dyed a deep dark green, the bodice picked out in pale gold thread. Deer and foxes were embroidered along the sleeves, and the fabric was softer than anything I'd touched since we left the city.

The second dress was red.

Color flashed across my mind. Roses in my mother's garden, blood spilled across snow, and last, absurdly, the Huntress's lips, her smile mocking my father as he raised his sword against her.

I folded it up hastily and shoved both gowns back to the bottom of the trunk, piling more garments on top of them. My hands paused over the wool tunic, leggings, and breeches. My own clothes were not suited to this cold. Feeling the stranger's eyes on me, I slipped out of my red skirt and folded it carefully, thinking about the red dress at the bottom of the chest.

I pulled on the wool stockings, leggings, and breeches, relief rushing in to fill the absence of my old clothes, which had smelled strongly of bear. In the city, women wore what they wanted, not like the cloying, backwater village I'd just left. My legs felt free without the skirt. I laced my boots up over the pants, wishing I had found a pair of sturdier boots in the chest as well. The green tunic fit, as did the soft, clean undershirt, and the sweater had a heavy collar that rested comfortably against my neck, promising to block out drafts of icy air.

Once on, the stranger's clothes made me feel a little better. Perhaps this was why knights made such a fuss about their armor. It wasn't just the physical protection it offered, but the act of girding oneself up for battle that made the difference. These new clothes felt braver than my old ones.

The door was unlocked, I knew. The tray of food I had retrieved was proof of that. All I had to do was open it, and then . . .

Then what?

Find someone.

The urgency in the thought had another cause. I had to use the latrine, and I had no desire to test the limits of the chamber pot I had found in my search of the tower room. I lifted the latch on the door, pushing past the panicked voice that warned the door would now be locked and I would be trapped here until I starved to death or froze.

It opened.

On the other side, curled up on the landing of the spiral staircase that went on in both directions, lay the white wolf.

I shut the door and threw my weight against it, panting. No sound came from the hall. It might have been the same wolf that had watched me from across the clearing. Then again, the features about the wolves that tended to grab my attention were their size, speed, and the length of their teeth. Aside from the black wolf, that didn't leave a lot of room for differentiation. They all looked huge, they were all unnaturally fast, and there was not a single one among them not in possession of teeth that could disembowel a lamb or a man in one snap. Now one of them was outside the door for reasons I could only assume were not in my best interests.

I lost track of how much time passed while I debated whether or not to risk opening the door again. Long enough for me to decide that the only thing worse than opening the door was remaining trapped in the room indefinitely while my bladder threatened to burst. I took a deep breath and lifted the latch.

The Huntress stood on the other side with her hand raised to knock. She looked just as surprised as I felt, green eyes widening as they took in my change of clothes.

"You ate," she said.

I glanced at the wolf beside her. Golden eyes met mine, revealing nothing.

"Yes."

You ate? That is all you have to say to me? I thought. Up close, we

49

were almost of a height, for all that she was broader through the shoulders and more powerfully built. She had seemed much larger standing beside the bear.

"Follow me." She turned and walked away, the wolf trotting at her heels.

My mouth shut slowly as she rounded the bend in the staircase, leaving me alone in the dark hall.

"Wait." I walked as quickly as I could after her, my boots making more noise than the Huntress and the wolf combined. "I need . . . I need the latrine."

She looked at me as if I had just spoken gibberish, then pointed toward a narrow door in the center of the staircase's spiral.

The latrine was spare, nothing more than a board over the long chute, but it had a mirror of polished brass hanging on one wall. I rubbed it with my sleeve. Tangled hair and wild eyes stared back. I tried to straighten my hair, then gave up. It was matted with sweat and long-since melted ice, and no amount of finger brushing was going to undo it. I needed oil, a hot bath, and a comb, none of which seemed likely. *You're as vain as Aspen, after all,* my reflection seemed to say. I licked my lips and braced myself for the sight of the wolf beyond the door.

I tried to keep track of our progress so that I could find my way back to the tower room which, now that I had left its confines, felt safe and secure, but the wolf trotting beside me drove all sense of direction from my mind. I tried to pretend it was a dog, but there was nothing dog-like about it; the paws were too big, the tail too short, the head too narrow, the snout too long. Every hair on its body rippled with predatory potential.

The corridors blurred together, lit by the dim light of the arrow slits. Shadows that might have been unlit torches and wall sconces passed me, but the Huntress moved with such surety that I half wondered if she could see in the dark like a wolf.

What light there was illuminated floors littered with dead leaves and the occasional bone, more like an animal's warren than a place of human habitation. It made my skin crawl. Despite the debris, the curious lack of dust persisted. Everything smelled cleanly of animal and snow.

Where are we going? I did not ask.

The keep seemed larger inside than it had looked from the frozen lake, and I wondered if she was intentionally trying to disorient me.

As we walked, the air grew warmer.

"In here."

The corridor came to an abrupt end. A large, stone archway opened into a dark space beyond, and the Huntress struck a spark against an oil lamp. It flared against my eyes, much brighter than it had a right to be, and she lit more lamps until the cavern sparkled. The walls were hewn from the mountain—that much was clear, and stalactites encrusted with crystal dangled from the ceiling. In the center of the cavern, encircled with black and white stones, stood three pools. They bubbled softly, and the air smelled faintly of sulfur.

"What . . .?" My question trailed off.

"Hot springs. The mountain keeps them warm. You may bathe if you wish."

A bottle of oil, a comb, and a towel lay by one of the pools. I stared at them suspiciously, wondering if she could read minds.

"I will return for you in an hour."

I listened to the faint whisper of her boots until they passed beyond hearing, leaving me alone with the weight of the mountain above me. I shivered. Steam rose from the water, and I thought about how vulnerable I would be, sitting naked while some unknown beast with fangs and claws prowled the cavern's depths, thirsting for blood.

An hour.

How long did she expect me to bathe?

I placed a hand in the water. It was hot, and felt faintly oily, like the public baths in the city. I withdrew my hand slowly.

I did not have to bathe. I could run, stumbling down the castle halls until something caught me. I could wait here, fully dressed

51

and dry, until she came back. Or I could sink below the surface of the water and breathe it in, ending this nightmare.

It was the last thought that made up my mind. I did not want to die here, but I stood a much better chance of convincing someone to help me if I looked presentable. I shucked off my new clothes and folded them carefully within reach, then bathed myself with a vengeance. I was dry, combed, and clean by the time she returned, hurried along by the thought of her eyes on my bare skin. She did not register any emotion at my improved appearance.

"Are you hungry?"

I wanted to go back to my room, where I could pretend to be brave.

"Yes," I said instead.

We went back up the stairs, coming again to the kitchen. "You don't eat in the hall?" I asked, remembering the tables shoved against the walls and the empty dais.

"I don't hold court. The kitchen is warmer."

"Where . . ." I took a deep breath and blurted out the question I needed answered most. "Where do the servants eat?"

She turned, and I nearly walked right into her. This close I could count the shadows of her eyelashes on her cheeks.

"Servants?"

"I thought . . ."

"You will not find any servants here. You will have to see to your needs yourself, my lady."

The mockery in her voice was unmistakable.

"That's not what I meant," I said, but then the meaning of her words sank in. If there were no servants, then who would help me?

"What did you mean?"

She was so close to me. I wanted to step back, but my body refused, rigid with terror.

"Is there anyone else here besides you?" I hated the desperation that leaked into my words.

Her eyes gleamed, as feral as her wolf.

"You're here," she said, and her smile cut deeper than the north wind.

Red berries on a dark limb.

The Huntress paused, the bear shifting beneath her.

Rowan.

She had never realized how many rowan trees grew in the mountains, or how bright the berries gleamed against the snow. They pricked the eyes like blood.

Fresh tracks beside the tree.

Deer. She could smell them, a faint musk that spoke of hunger and chewed bark. She moistened her lips, tasting the air.

Not far.

The branches of the rowan tree tangled in her hair as the bear lumbered forward. She tugged, and a few berries spilled into her lap.

They had served rowanberry jam with game. The sauce was bitter-sweet, a sharp tang against the honeyed roasts. Old laughter rang in her ears, and the remembered stench of sweating, breathing, feasting men and women overpowered the smell of deer.

She had sat with her Hounds at the high table. Masha—quick-tempered, first to throw words or knives. Neve—first to the ale, last to bed. Brendan—big-fisted, big-hearted, favorite among puppies and children. Lyon—faster on foot than a horse, but slow to laugh. And Quince. Small, sharp Quince, her shadow, her right hand, the last of her Hounds to fall to the witch's spell. Which of them had the hunters taken? Which of her kin had they cut down, with their crude crossbows and steel traps?

She threw the berries from her. They scattered on the snow like drops of blood.

53

The deer were upwind.

She slid off the back of the bear and hefted her spear. Without the bear's height, the berries faded from sight, and with them, the memories.

Snow, ice, thorn.

Within the briars, the Hounds lived on.

The witch smiled in the Huntress's memory. She broke into a run, her long stride swallowing the drifts, until the smell of the deer drove away all else.

Chapter Six

I pulled another carrot, the dirt crowding underneath my finger-nails. Carrots, in the middle of winter. The pile in the basket beside me grew. One onion. A handful of potatoes. A leek. Greens. Too many things that should not be, even with the glass ceiling filtering the pale sunlight as it lit the winter garden. My mother had taken me to the great glass greenhouse in the city, but this was nothing like that towering edifice.

Seven carrots total. One for each day I'd been here. I leaned back on my heels, staring around at the rows of plants. The pungent smell of crushed herbs clung to my fingers.

I was no closer to an escape than I had been that first day. If anything, I was farther, and the only thing I had managed to accomplish was to find my way from my room to the garden, the kitchen, and the baths. When I strayed beyond this narrow path, a wolf inevitably appeared around the next bend. They never snarled at me or came too close, but I was not stupid. I had been allotted my territory, and they guarded theirs. I felt like a sheep, and right now I even smelled like one, the steam from the spring in the corner of the garden leaving a fine mist over my wool tunic. As with the rest of the castle, the hot spring kept the garden from freezing, and I had come across warm pipes while digging. It would have impressed me more if I had not been a prisoner.

At least the garden gave me something to do. It was heavily overgrown and in need of a firmer hand than whoever had been tending it. Each day, I brought my small harvest to the kitchen, and each day the stew was there, meat broth bubbling, waiting for me to scrub and dice the vegetables. There were knives aplenty; the Huntress did not seem to consider me a threat. She hardly seemed to consider me at all.

I saw her, now and then, from a window or in passing. Once she carried a young deer over her shoulder, another time a brace of hares. Twice I came across her frowning at something out of sight, only to have that frown transferred to me.

"Tonight, she will speak to me," I told the carrots. They turned blank, orange faces towards me, their green tops brushing my forearms.

She was not in the kitchen when I entered, but the stew was there, simmering away.

"It would be nice to have something besides stew," I told the pot as I set about preparing my harvest. "A roast, maybe. With roasted potatoes and herbs and garlic."

The pot was as silent as the carrots, but the hair on the back of my neck prickled.

"I'll lay out some boar, then," the Huntress said.

I spun around, dropping the onion I was halfway through slicing onto the floor. Snow melted on her hair and shoulders, and her usual entourage of wolves ranged behind her, watching me with idle curiosity.

"Do you like boar?" she asked as I bent down to retrieve the onion. Thinly veiled mockery shone through her words. "Or would you prefer suckling pig? Maybe a rack of lamb?"

"Roast duck, actually." I sliced the onion more viciously than was necessary, her tone getting under my skin. "With candied cherries in a wine sauce."

Her lips twitched in what might have been a smile or a frown, and she pushed off from the door frame she had been leaning against to stand next to the fire.

"Wine, I have." She poured some into a small pot and set it over the flames. "Care for it spiced?"

"Um, yes, please."

At my halting reply, the mockery, and any trace of levity, vanished from her tone.

"Spiced it is then."

I took a chance. "I was wondering where the wine came from," I said.

"Someplace expensive, I expect."

I narrowly missed my finger with the knife. "My father served a similar vintage."

"He didn't seem like the sort to keep a table that could support it."

"He was a merchant," I said, my pride stinging.

"Was?"

"Well," I said, attacking a potato, "you don't think I ended up in that village by choice, did you? Shit." The knife nicked my finger.

She moved, quick as a cat, and pressed her sleeve against the cut to staunch the blood. After a week of nearly perfect solitude, her touch sent a shiver down my spine.

"You're not from the mountain?" she asked, examining the cut.

"It's my mother's village, but I was born on the coast."

"It was bad luck, then, that brought you here."

Yes, I thought. *A mountain of it.*

"Did your father have ships?"

"Three."

"This isn't deep," she said, releasing me. "But be careful shedding blood here. What did he trade?"

The casual way she mentioned blood set my heart racing, and I glanced at the wolves. None of them seemed to have scented my blood, but perhaps there were other, hungrier things about.

"Cloth, mostly." I tried not to let her see my fear. Animals could smell that, too. "He wanted to sell furs from the mountains after we fled the city."

Her silence warned me long before she spoke.

"A poor choice." It was all she said, but the temperature in the room dropped.

"It was," I said, rushing to fill the frigid air. "Nobody would touch his goods. That's why he needed the Locklands. He wanted to trade through them, but no city merchant would take someone from the mountains seriously. And now . . ."

"Now he trades bones for more bones."

It was an odd phrase, and I braced myself for the question I had to ask. "Did you kill them?"

"Who?"

"The other two men with my father."

The Huntress turned away from me and poured the wine into two horns.

"They knew the price."

"The price for what?" My voice rose. I tried not to think about the white wolf on the sledge and the resemblance it bore to her other wolves.

"Drink," the Huntress ordered.

I obeyed, but the wine did not drown my questions.

"The price for what?" I asked again.

She gave me a swift, piercing look. "You don't know who I am, do you?"

"You're the Huntress," I said, taking another sip. "But I don't understand what that has to do with a price. Or murder."

"If you knew who I was, you would not be asking me that question."

I felt my fear ebb, pushed aside by a growing wave of irritation.

"Fine. Are you going to tell me?"

She swirled the horn of wine, glancing up at me once through the tendril of steam rising from it.

"I haven't decided."

Before I could release my cry of outrage, she stood, beckoning me to follow her. "Come, merchant's daughter. I have a place for questions."

She led me up a different staircase. I thought it might lead to the central tower, but I was not sure. I had been allowed so little access to the keep that the layout remained hazy.

"I assume you can read?" she asked, coming to a halt beside a large door framed by lintels carved in the shape of massive bears.

I nodded, and then she opened the door.

My father had kept a small library in our town house. Three shelves: one for the histories, one for his records, and one that contained everything from epics to old sea charts.

This room was different.

Shelves lined every wall, and in the center stood a round hearth with a copper chimney. The grate around the fire was carved with more hunting scenes, but it was what the light of the fire revealed that held my gaze.

Books. More books than I could count, and scrolls and maps and even a table with a life-size model of the mountains. I stepped toward it, trailing my hand along the sharp peaks as my eyes devoured the room. I forgot about my father, and the Locklands, and the story behind the Huntress's name.

I had seen one other library like this, and that had only been a glimpse, on the solitary occasion my father had brought me with him to court. Books were expensive, and their contents hoarded. The wealth of knowledge in this room was staggering, and unlike the library at court this one did not have guards standing at attention to make sure the books remained untouched.

Well, unless I counted the wolves.

"There . . ." I trailed off and tried again. "There are so many of them."

"The winters are long here."

Out of the corner of my eye I saw her run a hand through her hair. It hung loosely around her shoulders, absorbing the torchlight, and it framed lips twisted in a smile that slashed her face in a cruel stroke.

I approached a shelf, my hand stretched out in preparation to touch the hide-bound spines. Some had titles marked in gold leaf; others were blank, their contents concealed by their bindings.

So many words.

A hunger that had lain dormant since we left the city woke. I chose a book at random, pulling it off the shelf and cradling it between my hands.

I'd taught myself to read. Sitting on my father's knee, watching him pore over lists and missives, I'd given him the surprise of his life when I corrected him. "Sheep, papa, not ship," I'd said, or so he told the story.

Not that it had done me much good. Women in the mountain villages did not need to read, and few enough men bothered with the skill.

But a library this size . . . Only royalty could command such a collection. Royalty, or a sorcerer.

I turned back to the Huntress, the book unopened.

"Who are you, really?" I asked. "You said this was a room for questions."

"I didn't say it was a room for answers." She crossed the space between us and pulled another book off the shelf, her fingers skimming the spines familiarly until they found the one they sought.

"Brother Bartleby. He was well traveled for a monk." She handed the book to me, then gestured around the room. "Help yourself to anything you want to read."

I tucked the book under my arm without looking at it, my body prickling with unease. I was not going to be distracted by Brother Bartleby.

I tried another tactic.

"So, what am I doing here?" She was still close enough that I could smell the melted snow on her hair.

"The same thing I am doing here," she said.

"And what is that?"

"I'm not a philosopher." Her voice had the high clarity of running water, but I heard the growl beneath the music. "Neither is Bartleby. That's why I like him."

She turned, her eyes on the door, and I grabbed her sleeve. She froze, looking as shocked as I felt at the boldness of my actions.

"Tell me why you have brought me here." My voice didn't shake, and her arm was warm and human beneath my hand, but there was nothing human about her eyes.

"A rose for a rose, a thorn for a thorn."

Cats had eyes that color. Green, hypnotic, predatory. My body tensed for flight.

"I am not a rose," I said.

She tilted her head. "Then perhaps you are a thorn."

My hand pulsed in a memory of pain, and I heard a distant rustle of leaves as my breath caught. I pulled my hand back, clenching my fingers tight against my palm as I tried to steady myself, but my heart beat too rapidly and the pain in my palm was sharper than the prick of the rose had ever been.

Something is wrong.

The books spun, then steadied, and I flinched as the hot wine sloshed over my shaking wrist.

"Drink," she advised.

I did, and the wine drove back the leaves from the corners of my vision but not from my mind. "I think I need some fresh air," I said.

She didn't say anything, and so I stepped past her, keeping my steps to a walk until I was through the doors. Only when I was sure she was out of sight did I break into a run, flying down the stairs and through the dark corridors until I was back in the kitchen, then the empty hall, and finally the stable. The open doors at the end framed the fading light, and I stumbled to a halt in the drifts, gasping down lungfuls of cold air.

A thorn for a thorn.

I would have preferred to be locked in a cell, I decided, staring at the roses rioting over the stone walls. I would have preferred to sleep on filthy straw and endure depravity after depravity, rather than this false freedom. I would rather have suffered at the hands of a brute, because that was knowable, predictable, and a simpler kind of fear. I would have preferred anything to the terror building slowly within me, along with gods knew what else. I pressed my bare hand into the snow, willing the cold to freeze away the throbbing pain.

I had imagined the rose moving in my hand. Hadn't I?

I had imagined the ice covering the kitchen table.

I had imagined all of this, and soon I would wake up, damp and weak from fever, because this was the stuff of madness and fever dreams.

My tears froze on my face, and my hand began to itch and burn with cold. I tucked it under my chin, wary about bringing it too close to my heart. I did not want anything else taking root.

The shadows cast by the walls climbed the keep as the sun set. I shivered. This was a cold I had never endured. It stopped my breath and burned in my lungs, and when I tried to stand at last my legs were heavy with it.

Dread rushed back into the space the cold had vacated. There was hot stew waiting, and wine and a library and a warm bed—all the things another me would have cried out with joy to receive only a few days ago. I looked back over my shoulder at the snow, now turning blue with evenfall.

They said it was the gentlest of deaths. You felt warm at the end, and sleepy. It would not take long. I took a step back toward the drifts, and then a growl broke into my thoughts. I jumped, my heart forcing blood back into my extremities. There was nothing gentle about being devoured. I tried to determine where the growl had come from, but all I could see was the settling dusk, and that the stable stood between me and safety. I hurried toward it. My eyes could barely make out the stone arches that demarcated the stalls, and I fumbled in my pocket for the flint I'd taken from the mantelpiece in my room as I felt along the wall for a torch, letting out a prayer of thanks when my hands found one.

It took several attempts for my frozen fingers to get a spark, and another several attempts before the torch lit. The light cast more shadows than it illuminated. When I was halfway to the door, I heard a yip coming from the next stall. I edged forward, holding my breath until I could peer around the edge of the stone. A pair of eyes caught the torchlight, and I made out the dark shape of the she-wolf hunched against the far wall and the handful of smaller shapes milling around it, mewling. Beneath the glowing eyes of their mother, I spotted glistening, bared teeth.

"Go no closer," said a voice at my shoulder.

I almost dropped the torch.

The Huntress raised her arm, placing it gently but firmly between me and the wolf.

The pups mewled louder at the Huntress's voice, a few bold ones attempting to cross the sea of straw and old bones between us.

"This way." She stepped back, waiting for me to follow, but the light of my torch had just fallen on another mewling shape. This one was only a few feet from my boots, lying prone on the exposed stone floor. Its little chest rose and fell so slowly I was not sure it breathed at all.

"What," I said, struggling to find my voice. "What about that one?"

The Huntress's eyes, like the she-wolf's, burned gold in the light of the torch.

"It is weak."

"Is it going to die?"

She knelt beside it, pressing a finger to its muzzle. It barely stirred.

"Yes," she said.

"And you're just going to leave it?"

"The mother did."

"But—" The pup tried to raise its head, belatedly recognizing the departed warmth for what it was.

"Life is cruel, and winter is crueler. The other pups will be stronger without it."

It let out a high, thin sound.

I recognized that sound. It was the whimper that had been building in the back of my throat for a week now, full of desperation and bewilderment.

"No."

I thrust the torch in front of me, moving before she could stop me, and scooped the pup up from the flagstones. The she-wolf let out a growl that threatened to rip muscle from bone, and I scrambled backward into the Huntress with the pup pressed against my breast.

The wolf held her ground.

I clutched the pup tighter to me as my heart knocked against the pup's fragile rib cage, momentarily grateful for the strength of the Huntress's body behind me, until I realized that she could feel the quickness of my pulse and the terror radiating from my pores. Animal instinct jerked me away, and I looked up into her face. She did not say anything, but her eyes wavered between green and gold.

The pup stirred enough to nuzzle my neck, and a grim certainty settled over me as its blunt muzzle searched along my jaw, the way it had in the weeks following my mother's death when I'd woken from grief to find my younger sisters' eyes glued to me from within their round faces, waiting for someone to tell them what to do now that the world had stopped ending and the sun was shining and the roses in my mother's garden were again in bloom.

A pup might die somewhere, someday, but not this pup.

The Huntress watched me. Torchlight cast the queer shadows on her face I was slowly growing accustomed to, and I tried to block out the sound of rustling leaves. At last she nodded, turning on a silent heel and leading the way back to the kitchen.

She remained silent throughout most of the meal. I ate quickly, the pup curled up in my lap. Her fur, for the pup was female, was dark and dull, and her bones felt fragile as eggshells. My conviction flagged, and the strange rustling at the edge of hearing threatened to drive me mad. She was not as small as I had first believed, but still small enough that I suspected milk was the best choice.

I had no milk.

I eyed the soft chunks of meat floating in the stew and tore a small strip off to feed to the pup.

"No," the Huntress said, green eyes lidded as she studied me with that quiet, unreadable look that I had seen so often in the eyes of her wolves over the past week.

"Then what should I do?"

"Give it here."

She held out her hands and I passed the bundle of fur to her after only a few moments of hesitation. Its wormy little tail wagged as it recognized her scent, and I inched to the edge of my seat, ready to snatch it back at the first hint of violence.

Instead, she nestled it in the crook of one arm, took a bite of stew meat, and began to chew methodically, her eyes never leaving mine.

"I don't—" I began, but then she put her mouth to the pup's, and I fell silent. The tail wagged some more, and the blunt muzzle lifted. I watched with my stomach turning as the Huntress let out a fine dribble of chewed meat. The pup lapped at it, first tentatively, then vigorously, and the Huntress spat the rest of the meat into her hand.

Revulsion warred with hope.

"You are lucky," she said, letting the pup nose through the brown slop. "It knows what solid food is."

I refrained from pointing out that chewed meat was hardly solid.

"So it will live?" I asked. My hands twitched, ready to take back the pup.

"It might. It is still young for weaning, and it may never be as strong as its siblings. You will need to feed it every few hours, and chew the meat. The mother throws it up," she added, perhaps sensing my distaste. She passed the pup back.

I stroked its skull, noting the round curve of the ears. "You will live."

"Rub its belly," the Huntress told me on the second day when she came across me trying to feed the pup more crudely chewed meat.

"Why?" I said, exhausted from a night of little sleep.

She knelt beside me, massaging the pup's taut abdomen with smooth, downward strokes of her thumb. "Because it can't eat if it hasn't shat."

Her head was bent towards the wolf, and I noticed the intricate knot that bound her hair at the nape of her neck. She smelled today of pine, not snow, and beneath the pine lingered a remnant of roses. My breath caught, and the world spun, then steadied, light frozen as it played over the smooth skin of her cheek.

"Here." She took my hand, mimicking the slow stroke. The pup squirmed, flailing paws that seemed larger today than they had been yesterday, and tried to mouth my fingers with the beginnings of needle-sharp teeth. I let her guide me, and I thought inexplicably of Sara.

"Like this," I had said, adjusting Sara's position on the quill as she struggled to form letters on the scrap of parchment I had smuggled out of my father's study.

"I feel like I'm going to break the damn thing," she'd said, staring at the quill in her calloused fingers.

I felt that way now, touching the pup's delicate skin, my eyes glancing off the Huntress's lips. *Nothing natural is that perfect,* I told myself.

At the nape of the Huntress's neck, tangled in that dark knot, I saw a flash of red. I reached for it, pulling my hand out of hers without thinking, and plucked the rowan berry from her hair.

She flinched at my touch, then stilled, her body taut, her breath silent. The berry rolled to the center of my palm and settled over the scar-that-wasn't-a-scar.

"There was something in your hair," I said in a voice so soft I barely heard it myself. She raised her eyes to look at my hand. It was the only part of her that moved.

The pup rolled over and began worrying the leg of my pants, but the Huntress remained kneeling, her eyes raised to mine, every muscle in her body tensed. I closed my hand slowly around the berry, my own breathing so shallow it barely brushed my lips.

One moment she was beside me, and the next the air was cold and empty and she was gone, her long stride taking her out of the kitchen and into the keep. I rose, hoping the pup did not choose that moment to defecate, and scrambled for the stairs. She moved with a speed that was impossible to follow at a walk, and so I ran, my footsteps ringing against the stone until the sound forced me to slow. The last I saw of her was a flash of bright silver as she mounted another flight of stairs. I stopped at the bottom, panting. This was the other tower, the one with the candle that burned against all logic, and the stairs climbed up into darkness. I sat at the foot, the pup mewling from the unexpected abuse, and did not follow.

Her skin burned where the girl's fingers had touched her.

Burned, and the cold did little to ease the pain of it.

The door was locked behind her, and the window was open, the ghost lamp burning near the sill. The roses bloomed around it in a white lake, save for the rose that ran through her veins, red as the blood of the wolves she could not save, redder than the blood of the men who'd died to avenge them.

How many years had it been since someone had touched her like that, thoughtlessly, without fear? How many winters had passed outside of this one while she paced the snows? How many springs?

The girl's face floated before her.

She had a half-tamed, feral look to her. It was hard to picture her in a city somewhere, her hair brushed smooth and her eyes calm. The girl had too much of the mountain in her to thrive anywhere else, and yet . . .

The Huntress recognized that look. She had seen it in her own eyes, the last time she had looked in a mirror, however many lost springs ago that had been. Reckless, hungry, wild. A wolf in a cage.

She knew a thing or two about cages.

Freedom will bring you no joy, because the price of freedom will be the loss of one you cannot bear to lose.

"No more," she said. A breath of wind rustled the rose vines, and she thought she heard the witch's laughter. "No more memories. No more words."

A rose for a rose, whispered the vines.

"What do you know of loss?" she asked the witch. "Who were you to judge me?"

69

The wind sighed.

The Huntress closed her hand around the nearest vine, willing the past to stay where she had left it, bleeding out in a bed of green spring moss.

She had found freedom, here in the snows. It was the kind of freedom that had to be taken, earned each and every day from the cold, but it was enough. It was more than enough. She still had her Hounds, and she still had her forests. Those were the things she could not bear to lose. Even if . . .

She stopped.

There was no even.

There was no if.

She would not let the witch unmake what had been made. There would be no spring, here. Spring brought only death.

The Huntress tore the vine from the wall, calling down the snows in a rain of rose petals.

Chapter Seven

I watched her ride out into the blizzard from my window. The snow parted once, and I saw dark hair stream out from a white hood, and then nothing.

Days stretched, and it was dark even in the garden with the wind scrabbling at the glass roof and throwing snow in through the arrow slits of the outer hallways. I found an old fur long enough to fashion into a cloak and ratty enough that the attentions of the pup did little to detract from its appearance. Not that I cared. It was warm.

The keep fell silent without the Huntress. The pack was gone, and the remaining she-wolf kept to her den in the stables. My pup waxed and waned, bright-eyed and playful some days, listless and lethargic on others. "You cannot die," I told her, shaking her gently as she turned her muzzle away from the food I'd chewed for her.

I had said the same thing to my mother.

"You can die," I amended, looking the pup straight in her blue eyes. "But I will be very, very disappointed in you if you do." The pup wiggled in my grip, desperate to lick my face.

On the fourth day of the Huntress's absence, my feet took me to the tower, and I paused at the foot of the stairs. No wolf blocked my way. Light and whirling snow spilled in from the arrow slits, leaving drifts on the steps. I tucked the pup under one arm and placed a tentative foot on the first step. When no other creature materialized, I took another, and another, climbing up past empty rooms with doors half open with a purpose that set my teeth on edge.

There was a room at the top of these stairs. I had seen it, coming in out of the snow that first day. A room at the top of the tower with a single lit candle, in a castle that had stood empty for days before our arrival. No candle burned that long, and candles did not light themselves. I would find answers there.

I had to.

I regretted carrying the pup. A few days of food in her belly had put weight on her bones, and my legs burned from the climb. It was no wonder the Huntress moved the way she did. If I climbed this many stairs on a regular basis, I too would lope with the easy grace of a mountain lion.

I smelled them before I saw them. A pale, half-remembered scent ensconced in ice.

They spilled through the next arrow slit, tight white buds and full blooms ghosting against the dark stone of the stairwell.

A rose for a rose, a thorn for a thorn.

I had kept my distance from the roses at the gates. These, though, would be impossible to avoid if I wanted to continue upward. The fragrance grew stronger as I drew parallel with them, wary of the long, raking thorns.

They were not like the roses in my mother's garden. The petals were smaller, denser, wilder than the heavy blooms she grew in the loose, black soil of the coast. The thorns, too, were longer, the sharp curves promising pain to any who dared brush them aside.

My father had plucked one of these roses.

I tried to picture it, ignoring the voice that warned against such thoughts. Him, covered in ice and shivering as he trudged alongside the Locklands. The roses, waving in the wind, impossible, beautiful, a gift from a land without mercy.

A gift for his daughter.

He had handed me into the heart of winter, leaving me alone to deal with its thorns. Had he known what he was bringing?

Rage flared, immediate, demanding.

I would have died. I would have thrown myself into the drifts, or perhaps a chasm, before I brought one of these flowers home to my daughters. I would have plunged the rose into my breast or, better yet, laid it and my life before the Huntress's feet. I would have died a thousand deaths before I gave such a rose to someone I loved. I sagged against the wall, staring at the briars ahead.

I had asked for the rose. He would have stumbled past them if I hadn't, and home to us, and together we would have dealt with Avery. Together we would have survived, as we had before. The roses trembled in the gale outside. I let them catch at my clothes as I passed, because what was one more thorn?

I mounted the last flight with leaden steps.

A door waited at the top. The wood was dark with age and bound with iron. I paused before it, catching my breath, and traced the metal with my eyes. It was worked into the shape of a vine, but the work lacked delicacy, as if it had been made by human hands instead of sorcery. Only the lock showed real craftsmanship, and that too was heavy-handed, putting more emphasis on the bolt than the design. I placed my hand upon the metal, my heart sinking.

It was locked.

I'd climbed halfway up the mountain for a locked door.

The pup wiggled, and I set her down, resting my forehead against the door. Whatever was beyond it remained out of my reach.

Unless . . .

Sara had taught me a thing or two about locks.

I slid a pin from my hair, grateful that I'd thought to put it up out of the way today, and slid it into the chamber. The pin grew cold to the touch, then shattered. Frost bloomed across the lock. A shard nicked my neck as I stumbled backward, and I barely caught myself on the uneven stone wall. The pup whimpered, a feeling I echoed wholeheartedly, and I raised a hand to my cheek to feel the place where another piece of shrapnel had grazed my skin.

Sara had said nothing about how to pick spelled iron.

73

I tucked the pup under my arm and fled, whipping past the roses and the library until I was back in the comparative safety of the kitchen where the only things that bloomed were dried herbs.

"Damn," I whispered into the crackling hearth fire. Then, when there was no response and the emptiness of the keep sagged around me, I said it louder. "Damn, damn, damn you all." My scream startled the pup but I did not care. I slammed my hands on the table, the screams building until the words jumbled into one long wordless sound, at once high and low, raw and shrill, shredding my throat and battering against my teeth until the world was subsumed in sound. I slumped against the hard wood, my lips sore and stretched and my throat ragged. I didn't know what exactly I had expected to find. A person perhaps, another prisoner like me. A hope I hadn't realized I was holding on to died with my screams. I was alone here. Truly alone.

I can't do this, I thought, staring around the deceptively docile kitchen with its pots and herbs and pleasant fires. I would not spend the rest of my life here, chopping vegetables and enduring the mood swings of a woman who could order her beasts to eat me without so much as a moment of warning. Her library was no substitute for companionship. All the books in the world could not replace what I had lost, but I still had one way out.

I locked the pup in the kitchen and waded through the snow in the courtyard, blinking at the light. The storm had lifted, leaving a sky so brilliant it hurt my eyes. The roses on the gate nodded at me in greeting, dark stems indistinguishable from the black iron. I pushed the gate, fearing that it too would be locked and knowing that if it was, I would throw myself upon the thorns, both iron and wood, and claw my way either through the gate or into the next world.

It opened.

No, it did more than that.

It sighed at my touch, and the leaves rustled, perhaps the leaves on the gate, perhaps leaves somewhere else, both distant and close, leaves that I wanted to strip from the stem and stomp into the bleeding earth. Past the gate, the snow danced in glittering spirals as it blew across the lake. I closed my eyes against the unbearable brightness and sank into the snow.

How long would it take, I wondered, for the blood to freeze in my veins? The air was so cold it hurt to breathe. Hours? How long before I slipped into a sleep from which I would never wake? They found men frozen, Avery had told me, with smiles on their faces. I would die here one way or another. Why not now? I nestled deeper into the snow and waited for my mind to come up with an argument against it, but all I heard was the wind, whistling as it blew flakes of snow across the lake.

I opened my eyes a long while later, animal instinct forcing my lids apart. The bear swayed its massive head from side to side, and from atop its back the Huntress watched me, straight as the spear she carried, her eyes wilder than they had been before she left, and her mouth set in a high, untouchable line below cheeks that could have shattered clouds.

And her eyes.

I had thought they were green, but this was a green so dark I felt the ground lurch beneath me, the last green at the heart of winter, a shred of life in a place hostile to all things tender and growing, the green of pine needles in shadow and moss frozen on the banks of mountain streams.

She slid from the bear's back. I didn't stir. The snow was soft, and if I didn't move, if I didn't reclaim ownership of the body in the drift, I could watch her a while longer from the frozen center of the world where everything was color and light and only cold demanded feeling.

"No." She held out her hand. No emotion crossed her face, but I knew that she knew what I was doing, lying in the drifts, and with that knowledge came everything I had tried to leave behind. The weight of the world pressed me deeper into the snow.

"Get up."

The growl in her voice lit into me like lightning. I grabbed her forearm, clumsy with cold, and stood.

She turned away to look out over the lake. A new bearskin

cloak hung around her shoulders, and the beast's claws crossed at the breast, the long, black nails nearly the length of my hand. What was left of its head hung at her back, a gore-stained hood with empty eyes still rimmed with red.

"I want to go home," I told her, the wind catching at my voice.

"You have no home," she said, as calmly as another person might have said, "dinner is ready," or, "I don't think it will rain."

"I do. I have two sisters, and—"

"That life is over."

I drew breath to argue, but the space between us was gone and the scent of the very-recently-parted-from-its-body bearskin overwhelmed me.

"Your life is not yours to throw away."

"What?" I looked up at her, hating her for the way she looked right through me without seeing me, hating her for her indifference, for her secrets, for the story she would not tell me and the life she had stolen from me without any reason I could see.

"You belong to Winter now." She fingered the claws crossed at her breast, and her gloves came away dark with blood.

"I belong to no one but myself."

"Don't you?" The scorn in her voice filled the space between us. "You are a debt, merchant's daughter, here to pay for your father's mistakes. If you throw your life away, I may consider that debt unpaid."

"Then kill me yourself and be done with it. Or do you really have no mercy?"

She laughed. The sound forced me back a step, and I stared at her as she threw back her head, her pale throat gleaming until the mountains rang with her mirth. "Your father asked for mercy, too," she said when she had finished. "But he was a fool. He did not understand what he asked for."

"Understand what?"

"Death is mercy in the mountains."

She was mocking me. I tore my eyes away from her and looked out over the mountains and into the clouds. "Give me mercy then."

"No."

"Then what am I supposed to do?" My voice cracked as I faced her, and more than I hated her, I hated the way my hand reached out, desperate, searching, grasping for something I would never find here in this cold, bright place.

"Live." She pulled her hand out of mine. Her mouth twisted again, but this time there was no cruelty in the line of her lips, and my hand ached where it had so briefly held hers.

"What is there to live for?" I asked her, pointing out at the wasteland around us. She turned to follow the accusation in my fingertips. Her face eased, and the tautness in her shoulders lessened as her eyes took in the distant line of pines and clouds and falls of ice. She didn't speak, but I saw the answer in the way her lips softened, parting slightly as a breath of snow danced along the lake. A hawk circled, spinning a trail of frost as it dived in and out of the clouds at our feet. I wanted to deny the beauty of her world. I wanted to deny the ache that had spread from my hand to my chest, tightening like a fist the longer I looked at her lips. I wanted to hate her, and I wanted her to look at me the way she looked at her mountains.

"There's nothing here worth living for," I said, summoning up the remnants of the vitriol still churning in my stomach.

She turned back to me and the tightness returned, sliding over her body like a second skin as the sweep of her cloak stirred the snow. My cheeks flamed in the cold as she walked away.

"Damn you," I called after her.

She looked back over her shoulder, the bear fur framing her cheek, and gave me a smile that froze the air around it.

"I am already damned."

Pain.

She saw it in his eyes, and she lay her hand against his head, smoothing the fur over his ears. The cuts were deep. She hummed softly under her breath, and with her other hand she held the cloth to his side to staunch the bleeding.

"I am sorry, my friend."

He whined.

This one was one of Brendan's grandpups, or great-grandpups. She had lost track, running with the wolves, of who they'd been. It hadn't seemed important. Each wolf was its own, and they were all her Hounds.

It mattered now. It always mattered right before she lost one.

The loss of one you cannot bear to lose.

"The things we can bear then," she said to the wolf and to the witch. "The things we can bear are terrible enough."

The wolf sighed, pain taking its toll on his body, and she closed her eyes against the grief. Sometimes she wondered if she loved them more, these pale shadows of the human hunters they had been.

She did not think of the girl.

She did not think of the despair she'd seen in those dark eyes, the snow so bright around them, and she told herself she did not feel regret like a hammer, striking again and again and again.

"Would that we all were wolves," she said to the wolf as pain from her own wounds clouded her vision until she slumped beside him, her hand on his bloodstained chest.

Chapter Eight

We had received the news at three o'clock in the afternoon, shortly after the striking of the bell. My father was in his study upstairs, and Aspen and Juniper were picking up the day's groceries as it was the housekeeper's day off. With the housekeeper gone, it fell to me to answer the door. I knew as soon as I saw Henrik's face that something terrible had happened. His white-blond mustache did not conceal the grim set of his lips, and he was out of breath and sweating.

"Your father," he said, looking past me. "Where is he?"

"Upstairs," I answered, but I blocked his way before he could push past. "What is wrong?"

Henrik gave me a long look, his ice-blue eyes fierce and pitying. "Everything."

A gust of wind whistled over the battlements, breaking through the shroud of memory. The wind must have sounded like that, I thought, out there on the water, shrieking as it ripped the sails from the masts, then the masts from the ships, and finally tore apart the ships themselves, timber by timber, leaving only a few broken casks and the half-drowned body of the cook's boy, the sole survivor of the gale that sank my father's three best galleons on their voyage home. All three were heavily laden with silks and spices destined for my father's clients, and it was only ill fortune that had them returning to our city at the same time, wallowing low in the water with their holds full of uninsured goods.

Damned.

Damned, indebted, and condemned.

I had thought the worst had happened before, first when my mother died, and then again when those ships sank, and lastly in an exile that ended at the dirt road wending its way through the foothills, grass growing in the ruts that led to the small cottage at the edge of the village. I had been ready to accept my share of the burden, wed to Avery and shackled to a town I despised while I grew old and my fingers gnarled and knotted, and our children rolled in the dirt with the dogs and I nurtured hate for my husband like an old bitter seed.

I had thought I knew the shape of loss.

This, though.

This was different. This was a rent in the fabric of reason. People simply were not carried off into the night on the backs of bears by women without a shred of human decency.

"I am damned."

If she was damned, what did that make me?

Cold, whispered the part of myself that paid attention to such things.

I left the ramparts, where I had come to brood, and headed for the hot spring. If there was any justice in the world I would be able to scrub away my grief in peace.

I found the cavern dark and empty. *Good*, I thought, stripping down out of my clothes and ignoring the pup, who scampered off into the shadows. I should have minded the darkness now that the Huntress was back. Anything could be lurking. If I lit the torches, however, I would have to see my reflection on the surface of the steaming pool.

I slid beneath the water, letting it run through my hair and over my shut eyes and lips. The warmth held me, and its touch was almost human. I ignored the tears that mingled with the water and waved off the pup, who had settled down next to me to gnaw on my ear. She was not so easily deterred. Sighing, I lowered my head until only my lips and nose floated above the water, removing myself from her reach.

This time of day at home I would be spinning, or perhaps wandering the village to put off the long companionable silence of the looming winter evening.

No.

Any dissatisfaction I may have had with the village could be surmounted if only I could return. I could get used to Avery. I could get used to a life of mindless superstition, sitting around the hearth and telling stories of harsh winters past.

My mind trembled, trapped between the worlds.

There had to be a way out.

I let the water work the knots out of muscles tight with anger and tried to think, pushing down the unease that thoughts of returning to Avery Lockland stirred.

The Huntress was back. However much I wanted to hate her, I could not escape alone. I needed more information about why I was here and where in the hundred thousand hells we were, and to do that I needed to find a way to actually *get* information.

The library.

I jerked out of the water, startling the pup, and almost laughed. I had a library right here. Surely somewhere in one of the scrolls was something I could use if I only knew what to look for. I had been an idiot not to see it before; there had to be some sort of record in the library of this place, and if not, the library's contents should be able to tell me something about the people who built it. I could begin my search tonight. The anger I'd felt earlier ebbed and the comfort of purpose settled over me, reassuring in its weight, until a fall of torchlight blinded me. I threw a hand over my face to shield my eyes and felt the surge of hope shatter around me, leaving me naked and raw in the curling steam.

"I—," she said.

I opened my eyes to find the Huntress staring at me with her mouth slightly open as she failed to finish her sentence. She wore only a cloth, and the torchlight fell on her bare shoulders and loose hair with more charity than the harsh glare of the winter sun. It made her look soft, almost vulnerable.

The illusion lasted no longer than the time it took the breath to catch in my throat.

"I did not mean to startle you," she said, her voice once again cold.

I said nothing. My lips were dry despite the steam wreathing my face, and I had never felt more exposed in my life.

The light fell across her back as she turned to leave. I gasped. Four deep gouges parted the flesh over her shoulder blades. "What happened to you?" I asked.

"Bear." She shrugged, then winced as blood seeped from the wounds. I thought of the bearskin cloak she'd worn on her return, and the long claws dangling from the skinned paws.

The sweat prickling my brow had nothing to do with the heat of the spring and everything to do with the layers of parted skin before me. I was out of the water before I could change my mind, clutching the linen to my chest. She should hardly have been able to walk with damage like that, let alone ride.

Leave her, I told myself. *She stole you from your home. Let the wounds fester. Let her rot and watch while the wolves rip her carcass limb from limb.* My stomach heaved. Without the Huntress, there would be nothing to keep the wolves from turning on me.

"Hold still," I told her, water streaming down my back from my wet hair. My hand shook as I placed it gently on the bare skin beside the gash. Leaves rustled, but I could barely hear them over the pounding in my ears. Her skin was hot to the touch, but not feverish, and smoother than mortal skin had any right to be. My thumb brushed the line of her shoulder blade without my volition, and I shook my head to clear it.

"It's nothing," she said.

I slid the towel down toward her hips, my eyes tracing the long, vicious curve of the wounds, and disagreed. "This needs to be sewn up and cleaned."

"I said it is nothing." I had never seen a beast caught in a trap, but with her lips half curled in a snarl and the whites of her eyes flashing, she reminded me of nothing more than that. *Let her die then,* I thought. I was no healer.

My palm seared, and something inside me unfurled. The sensation made me dizzy. I swayed as the torchlight flared.

"Rowan." She steadied me, the feral look gone from her eyes, and her hand burned on my shoulder. *She stole your life*, I told myself as heat rushed to my face. *She took everything from you.*

That did not explain the terrible longing that spread from her fingers like a fever.

"At least let me clean it then," I said, because anything was better than the lingering echo of tenderness in the way she'd said my name.

She stared at me for the space of several heartbeats, then nodded. "The water will loosen the worst of it," she said as she dropped the towel and stepped gingerly into the pool. I shut my eyes, still half-blind from the light, but the sight of her body seared the back of my lids like flame.

She hissed as the water hit the wounds. I knelt beside the pool and put my hand on her uninjured shoulder before I could stop myself. The dark water washed away the blood from the cuts, revealing several layers of muscle and a flash of white that I hoped was not bone. The skin around it puckered angrily, severed as smoothly as if the bear had wielded a knife instead of claws. I had never seen a wound like that on a living person. It hurt to look at. Her muscles knotted beneath my palm, and I saw a muscle leap in her jaw as she clenched her teeth against the pain.

"How can you bear it?" I asked in a hushed voice.

She sank deeper into the water, leaning her head against the stone floor. It was disconcerting to find myself looking down on her. Her eyes were half-closed, the lids bruised with an exhaustion that looked decidedly human, and the dark water covered her chest and pooled in the hollows along her collarbone. One of the gashes curved over her shoulder. I found myself wondering if it would scar, or if she healed with the same flawless ease as her roses.

"Pain is not so hard to bear," she said, looking up at me. "Just takes a little practice."

I laid the back of my fingers against the skin below her wound, checking once again for heat. "Have you had a lot of practice?"

"You could say that." Her lips curved in a smile that turned into a grimace as my finger brushed the edge of the gash.

"I'm sorry." I pulled my hand away.

"Don't be."

She closed her eyes, and I sat with my hands pressed tightly together, willing myself not to touch her or to stroke the damp hair back from her forehead. "Was it a large bear?" I asked to break the silence.

"Large enough."

"I thought bears hibernated." *Except hers, of course.*

"They do. This one was sick. Something drove it out of its season, and I did not want it killing my Hounds. Even a sick bear can kill a wolf." Her voice tightened on the last words.

"Or a hunter."

"I was careless. It happens occasionally."

I had a hard time picturing this woman performing a single careless act. Even now, submerged in water and her skin in tatters, she carried herself with more grace than I could hope to achieve in a lifetime.

"Have you lost many wolves?" I said, registering her words.

"I lost two to your villagers this past month, and tonight I may lose another."

Her face did not move, and her voice was even, but there was pain there beneath the ice. I remembered the pelts piled high on the sledge and a realization rose from the corpses like the steam from the pool. "That was the price. That's why you killed them. A life for a life."

"Yes."

"Is the life of a wolf the same? Those men had families. Wives."

"It is the same to me." She opened her eyes in time to see me shiver, the towel doing little to ward the chill off my skin. "Leave me," she said, her eyes almost black against the water. "If you truly want to help, start heating the wine."

85

Her blood stained the water of the pool.

Pain.

It was one of the things that bound her, her blood a reminder that all things could feel, all things could suffer, and nothing the witch had done could change that.

Now, as the steam rose and white stars burst in the cavern depths, she wondered how much of this the witch had foreseen. Perhaps the girl would have come anyway, even if she had killed the father. Perhaps it was woven into the fabric of her prison that she would never be at peace, and that always the mountain would rise, sending another of its envoys to the heights to break what should be left unbroken.

I could have brought winter down on all of them.

The thought drove away the pain, filling her with a savage longing. She could have let him keep the rose. She could have let it take root, there in that scrap of a cottage on the edge of Lockland land, and put out tendrils of frost, eclipsing all hope of spring.

She smiled, the bitterness rising like bile.

She could have driven cold into the marrow of their bones before the end, regardless of the cost.

Instead, she had Rowan.

Chapter Nine

The Huntress winced as the hot wine hit her back. I winced with her. The wounds looked even worse in the light.

"Give me the wine," she said, taking a long swallow when I handed the jug to her. I sopped up the last of the boiled wine in the wounds with a clean rag as she drank, my hands still shaking. I was beginning to regret my offer. This was far beyond my skill to heal.

"This would be easier if you were on the table," I said for the third time.

"Fine." She snarled the words but at last obliged me, laying herself out on the wood with her face averted. Half dressed, the skin of her back gleamed in the firelight, and the coppery smell of blood mingled with the scent of bath oil and pine. I eyed the needle and suture before me, glad that she could not see my unease. I had never sutured skin before, and I had a feeling it was going to be very different from leather or cloth. I took a sip of wine to steady my nerves, then took another.

"Do you want something to bite down on?" I asked.

"No."

I swallowed, my throat already dry again, then threaded the needle with the line.

"Why are you helping me?" Her voice was flat, and all I could see of her expression was the tension in her shoulders.

"I don't know," I answered, the truth slipping out. "But if it festers and you die, I'm dead, too."

"So, you have decided to live?"

"I have decided I don't want to be eaten by that bear of yours."

She made a sound that might have been a laugh. Like this, prostrate on the table with her face hidden, I could almost forget that I did not know what she was. *You've been alone for too long*, I told myself. *Do not be fooled by beauty, or by blood.*

"What convinced you?"

"This," I said, pushing the needle through. The feel of her flesh parting made my stomach churn, and I nearly lost my nerve. The Huntress held unnaturally still until I tied off the first stitch, but sweat sprang to the surface of her skin. "What would you have done without me?" I asked, forcing myself to breathe. Looking at the wound was making my head spin.

"Curled up in a ball until it healed enough to let me throw a spear."

"And if it hadn't healed?"

"It would have."

I threaded the needle again and begged to differ. Wounds like this could be fatal.

"I've received worse," she said, reading my thoughts.

Her skin, aside from the rents, was smooth and unblemished without so much as a birthmark, let alone a scar. I ran my hand along one of the muscles of her back, bracing myself to place the next stitch. My breath sounded very loud in my ears. I shoved the needle through again and whimpered.

"Rowan." The Huntress sat up, placing her hand over mine and taking the needle from me. I stared at it, trembling, willing myself to stop shaking. Skin was just leather. I could do this. I had to do this because there was no one else. Would never be anyone else for as long as I lived, trapped here on a distant mountain unless I could find my way back to a home I was not entirely sure I wanted.

"Let me help you," I said, my voice steadying. "Please."

Her hand tightened around mine at the last word and I looked at the ground, not wanting to meet her eyes. Without meaning to, I could see the firm line of muscle on her stomach, and below that the slight curve of her hips. She was as lean as her wolves, but in the firelight that leanness had turned into something far more dangerous.

It is magic, just like the lock at the top of the stairs. Just like the roses. Magic, not feeling.

"Rowan." She said my name again. I knew with devastating certainty that what I saw in her eyes in that moment would haunt me the rest of my life, no matter what else passed between us, no matter how deep my hatred, no matter how many years and leagues separated me from this place.

"Turn," I told her. The needle slipped in my hand and I caught it, staring at the bright tip. Leaves rustled. The quiet space I'd found in the snowdrift crept in and I stared at my palm. It remained unblemished, but there was an odd feeling, like building pressure, where the thorn had pierced me. Ignoring it, I placed my hand over the longest of her gashes, trying to count the number of stitches I would have to brave to finish what I'd started, and feeling foolish and fearful and all too aware of the unreal rustling that never strayed far from the edges of hearing.

My palm itched.

My palm burned.

Something in me *moved* and then a white-hot lance of pain shot out of my hand and into her shoulder. The Huntress threw back her head in agony and I tried to pull my hand away, but it was bound to her by a snaking vine of thorns.

"Don't. Move," she gasped.

As if I could move.

As if any of this were possible, or even within the realm of reason. The thin, green shoot sprouted thorns as it grew into her flesh, long and curving and black where they pierced her skin, and then they tightened, a mockery of my efforts to sew her up.

Then it was over.

I lifted my hand slowly, staring at the small, red dot of blood at the center and trying not to look at the tangle of briars on her back. Her breathing steadied. I clung to the sound, my eyes transfixed by the impossibility of what they had just seen.

"Rowan."

I looked up from my hand. The Huntress stared at me with a horror I felt mirrored in my bones. A strange sound filled the kitchen, a high thin chattering that stopped, for a moment, when I bit my tongue, blossoming into pain and copper in my mouth as my teeth resumed their chatter. At least the sound drove out the rustling leaves.

Bile rose in the back of my throat, and I held my hand as far away from my body as I could, as if by distancing myself I could deny the thing that lived within me. Gray crowded the corners of the room, gathering like snow clouds.

"No," I tried to say, but the noise I made was hardly human. I backed away from the Huntress, no longer seeing her, seeing only the red dot at the center of my palm while my other hand scrabbled behind me until it found what it was looking for. I raised the knife I used to chop vegetables and brought it down into the soft meat of my hand, feeling nothing and seeing only the vine, black in the firelight, snaking up the Huntress's back. I raised the knife again, searching, convinced that if I could find it, if I could pluck the thorn from my poor, violated flesh, I would wake up and this would all have been a nightmare.

She stopped me as I raised the knife for another blow. I strained against her, blood flowing down my wrist, my screams flaying my abused throat until the warmth of her bare shoulder pressed against my mouth and the knife clattered to the floor as she pulled me hard against her, trapping my wounded hand between us as my screams subsided into sobs.

"I want to go home," I whispered into the shadow of the Huntress's neck when the sobs, too, faded. She stroked my hair and did not answer, but I heard her thoughts as clearly as if she'd spoken them into my ear.

She could never let me go, now, even if she wanted to.

Another sob shook me. When it passed, I felt the weight of

91

her chin resting on my head, and I gradually became aware of the heat of her body, real and solid, a barrier between me and the roses on her back and the ice lodged somewhere deep within me. My heartbeat slowed to match hers.

I shivered when she pulled away at last, feeling newly exposed, as if the Huntress, terrible as she was, had held off something more terrible still. I must have made a sound, a whimper or some other pathetic animal plea, because her hand went to my cheek with a tenderness I had only ever seen her show to her wolves. I leaned against it. She might have brought me here, but she had not handed me the rose.

"If I had known what he would do, I would never have let your father live," she said, her tone gentle. "It is death to pluck them. The rest of your village knows that."

"Then why didn't you kill him?"

She gave me a sad little smile. "When I found him again, I thought I might. And then I saw you."

I blinked at her, my eyes raw and my body aching. "You asked me if he'd given me the rose."

"I wasn't sure then if it had taken root. Later, I thought I'd been mistaken, but that wasn't why I took you." She removed her hand, and my cheek burned with cold without her touch. "I took you because your father loved you, and because the only thing crueler than losing one you love is living with that loss. Death would have been a mercy."

I should have felt something at her words. Instead, I felt empty. Numb. "Will I die?" I asked her.

"Not from this," she said, lifting my hand to examine the damage I'd inflicted on myself. "And not by my hand, or by yours, if I can help it." That strange, sad smile was still on her lips. "And not by briar. They are just thorns, Rowan, and roses. Nothing more."

The wolf rested his head in her lap. He had decided to live through the night, despite his wounds.

"And I have lived despite mine," she told him.

She had thought she would rage against it, when the time came. She had thought she would fight it tooth and nail, snarling with her pack around her, not curled up like this, roses in her back, a wolf in her lap and a stranger's name on her lips.

Rowan.

She saw the elegance of the witch's trap. It had been there all along, and she had sprung it with one act of mercy. She should have killed him, she thought for the hundredth time.

But she hadn't.

". . . its blossoming will mark the end of everything that you now hold dear."

"What will become of you?" she asked the wolf. "What will become of you, when all this comes undone?"

He closed his eyes, his tongue lolling as he panted, and didn't answer. She let her hand rest above the soft curve of his ear.

There was nothing to rage against.

She remembered the way the girl had felt, sobbing in her arms. She remembered the way she smelled, and the feel of her hair, and the odd tightening she had felt in her own chest as Rowan's fear and grief spilled down her breast.

She did not know what came next. She had never fully understood the witch's words, and it was far too late now to ask, but she knew one thing for certain: she could not kill the girl, even if so doing could save her. Even if it meant the end.

"Even if it meant your life?" she asked the wolf. "What would I choose then?"

She didn't have an answer, only the smell of steel as a long-rusted trap sprang shut.

Chapter Ten

She found me in the library the next day. I was in the middle of a hide-bound journal, half of which had been destroyed by time, water, and something that might have been blood—but the last passage I'd read lingered in my mouth.

At the head of the hunt rode the King's huntress, a maiden unlike any I had seen in the lowlands. I did not realize, at first, that she was the King's daughter. The women here are as hard as their men—some harder—and for all that the girl could not have been much older than sixteen, the other hunters deferred to her. She rode as though she had been born on horseback with a hawk on her wrist, and she had the kind of face men broke themselves against. The prince was no exception. I have never seen a man fall so hard or so fast.

The pup pricked her ears toward the door, ceasing her attempts to mangle the carpet long enough to alert me to the Huntress's arrival. I clutched the book I had been reading to my chest, unsure of what to say to her after all that had passed between us the day before. She walked carefully, and there was an edge to her jaw as she bent to toss the pup a scrap of meat that suggested she, too, was aching from her wounds.

"Shouldn't you be resting?" I asked, glad of an excuse to break the silence.

"No."

"But your back . . ." I closed my eyes, wishing I could forget about her wounds and, more importantly, the briars.

"But your hand," she said, taking the book from me.

I opened my eyes, catching the gentle mockery.

"Look." She set the book down and began to unbutton her shirt. My mouth went dry, and dread mingled with something else as she slid her shoulder free. I became aware, in a way I had not been the day before, that she had been half-naked the last time I had touched her.

"Give me your hand."

I held my good hand out to her, and she raised it to the briar that curved over her shoulder.

"Thorn. Leaf. Stem."

I felt each as she moved my fingers over them, the thorns just scraping my palm, the leaves a soft brush of half-furled green, and the stem smooth where it lay along the red seam of the wound.

"Say it." She moved my hand in another pass.

"Thorn, leaf, stem," I said, naming each. I shuddered, and she tightened her grip.

"Say it again."

"I don't understand."

"Thorn, leaf, stem. Ice. Snow." She loosened her grip on my hand, and I let it fall, hesitating just once on the tip of the vine where a miniature rosebud rested like a jewel. "Be afraid of the things you can't name. The things you can't see. Like the lynx behind you."

I jumped, craning my head to see over my shoulder. "Where?"

"On top of the bookshelf."

I looked up and up and up, the shelves blurring until I saw the wildcat. Its ears twitched in sleep, and one paw hung off the edge, relaxed and almost as large as my fist. When I looked back at the Huntress, I could have sworn I saw her hide a grin.

"The lynx didn't come out of my hand."

"Luckily for both of us." She tried to tug the collar of her shirt back over her shoulder, then cursed in pain as it caught on a thorn and tugged at the wound.

"You deserved that," I said, feeling a little more like myself.

"Perhaps. Seven hells." She cursed again as the fabric caught a second time.

"Let me." I brushed her hand away before she undid whatever it was I had done in the first place and pulled the cloth up and over the thorns. As I straightened the collar of her shirt, the tips of my fingers slid along the smooth skin above her collarbone, and this time the hiss of breath took me by surprise. Her hand shot out, stopping mine, and something that wasn't pain moved behind her eyes.

"Don't," she said. Her voice was lower than I had ever heard it, more growl than speech, and the world narrowed down to a single pair of green eyes.

I felt my breath catch. "I'm sorry," I said, but my fingers burned where they still touched her skin, and I found myself wondering what I would have thought if my father had betrothed me to this woman instead of Avery Lockland. I had a vivid image of the Huntress lounging inside the Lockland lodge, polishing her hunting horn. It was ludicrous, and yet there were similarities, of a sort, between this woman's arrogance and Avery's.

Except her arrogance made my heart beat a little faster, and I would never have willingly stood this close to Avery. I pulled my hand away slowly. She let me go, but I found I could not step away from her.

"Do you miss the ocean?" she asked.

I didn't know what to say to that, and so I said nothing, looking up into her eyes while something that might have been distant surf or my heartbeat thundered in my chest. I nodded, mute.

"Good."

At the far end of the library, tucked in an alcove I had overlooked before, was a small table. The Huntress piled several scrolls on top of it, and I tore my eyes away from the muscles in her arms as she spread the first across the table.

I leaned in, transfixed. The map was beautifully drawn in colored inks that rippled over water and shore, and my eyes devoured the unfamiliar coastlines. Not even my father had owned a map like this. "It's beautiful," I said, running a hand along borders the artist had rendered in elegant loops and twists that brought to mind currents and waves.

"Is that what it looks like?"

"What, the ocean?" I began to laugh, and then I saw her face. She was serious. "In a way, I guess. It's blue. But . . ." I trailed off, picturing the sea's many faces. "It's blue like snow is white, or winter is cold. Blue is just a word. It doesn't do it justice. And it's not always blue. Sometimes it's gray, or even black, and when the sun hits the water it turns gold and the froth on top of the waves is as white as cream. And it sounds like wind in the pines. I used to wake up when I heard the pines in the village, thinking I was back home." I broke off.

"They say there are monsters in the waves," she said, pointing to a beast with too many fins, drawn in exquisite detail.

"There are monsters everywhere." I met her eyes. "But there are wolves in the water. Sailors have seen them."

"Wolves?" She rolled up the map, arching an eyebrow in disbelief, and opened another scroll. This one contained a drawing of a ship.

"That's a pirate ship," I said, pointing at the narrow hull. "You can tell by how it's built. They're fast. They have to be."

"All scavengers are fast."

"My father lost his cargo to pirates once."

"Are you sure it wasn't sea wolves?"

I glared at her. "If it had been sea wolves, they would have taken the men, not the gold."

She leaned against the table, watching me. I felt a flush creep up my neck under the scrutiny. "I wanted to see the ocean once," she said.

I tried to picture her standing on a wharf or striding across the deck of a ship, the wind snatching at her hair. I couldn't. She was ice and snow and mountains. "Why didn't you?" I asked.

"A hundred reasons, and then it didn't matter." She touched the parchment.

"Who were you, before you were the Huntress?"

She looked up, and I saw another woman in her face, a flicker of longing and loss. "Someone else."

"I think I would have liked to meet that person," I said, surprising myself.

A shadow fell across her eyes. "I am glad you didn't."

"Why? How could you be—" I cut myself off before I finished the sentence, but she heard the words I hadn't said. I could tell by the icy calm that descended once again over her features.

"How could I be any worse than this?"

"I didn't mean that," I said, wondering at the truth in my words.

"You haven't met many monsters, have you?" she asked.

I thought about the bankers in the city, with their cold calculations and unflinching exactness as they stripped everything of worth from my family. "I've met a few," I said.

"And your betrothed? Is he a monster?"

I felt her words like a slap. "Avery?" I asked, my world tilting. I had not told her about Avery. By not speaking his name out loud, I had kept these worlds separate, safe, protecting myself from acknowledging the things I did not grieve and, worse, the shimmer of relief I had found at the bottom of my despair. She reached into the slim pouch she wore at her belt and pulled out the carved wolf.

"Avery," she said, turning the carving over in her hands. "Is that his name?"

"How did you know I was betrothed?"

"This is a traditional betrothal gift, Rowan. Although he carved it with more skill than power, unfortunately for you. You're having quite the wolf winter."

I forced myself to breathe. It didn't matter in the end if she knew about Avery. "He's not a monster." I owed him that, at least.

"Do you love him?"

I laughed. The sound seemed to startle her, and her pupils contracted.

"No." I bit off the words. "No, I don't love him." *I will never*

99

love him. I am not capable of loving him, I thought. *Not like I loved Sara. Not like I could love someone like you, if you weren't the Huntress. If you weren't made of ice.*

Leaves rustled a warning.

She looked up. Her eyes filled half the room, and there was a wildness to the high planes of her cheekbones that set the hairs on my arms on edge. *"A wolf pup is not a dog, for all their similarities,"* she had told me when she had caught me trying to train the pup to sit for a scrap of meat. *"She will always be her own master. Never forget that. She may sit for you now because she feels like it and because it pleases you, but never forget what she is. She is wild; you will never know her heart, and she will never come to heel."*

What about you? I wondered. *Are you a woman, or are you too like your wolves?*

"Here," she said, handing back the wooden wolf. "I should not have taken this from you."

I accepted the carving. It felt oddly heavy in my hands.

"Avery Lockland," I said, stroking the little wolf's blunt snout. "You killed his father and brother, you know."

An unfamiliar expression flitted across her face. "I killed poachers. I did not ask them their names."

"Avery is the head of his clan now." I tucked the wolf into a pocket, half-wishing she had kept it. I did not want to think about Avery. I did not want to think about what he might do, as chieftain, to avenge the loss of father, brother, and bride.

"Perhaps he'll learn from their mistakes."

"I doubt it." *Ask me more about the sea,* I thought. *Anything that isn't Avery.*

"Do you think he will come looking for you?"

"No." I squared my shoulders. "I think he will be happy to be rid of me."

"And yet you would return to him."

"I would return to my family. If that means I have to marry Avery . . ." I trailed off, unwilling to finish the sentence.

"We do terrible things for the people we love." Her words reached in and shaped my panic.

"And we do terrible things *to* the people we love," I finished for her, thinking of my father. "Were you ever betrothed?"

"No."

It was a stupid question. She was the Huntress. She probably would have devoured the heart of the first man foolish enough to beg her favor. I remembered the woman in Avery's story, then dismissed the thought.

"I had my first suitor when I was thirteen. They were relentless." She touched her shoulder, grimacing. "First my mother said no, and then my father, and by the time it was up to me I'd learned the only answer I was willing to give."

"Where are they now? Your parents?"

"Somewhere in the snow." Something in her tone told me that was the only answer I was ever going to get. "I'll let you get back to your reading," she said, leaving me with my head full of ships and wolves and men I wanted to forget.

"*Lockland,*" *the girl had said. The word echoed in the empty hall-way, and there was a bitter taste in her mouth. Irony perhaps. Or hate. She'd tasted too much of both to remain discerning. Hot, bitter copper. The blood of winter.*

How many years had it been, she wondered, since she had tasted anything else?

How many years had it been since there had been anything else to taste?

The sky flashed through an arrow slit—blue, as blue as the eyes of the boy she'd killed. Things had been simpler when all she had wanted had been sharp teeth and soft flesh. Before the voice in her head had started speaking again, taking control of her tongue and twisting it into words she'd long forgotten.

Words. Words were the currency of memory, and yet even without them she had never really escaped those eyes.

"*I have paid,*" *she told the witch. "I have paid for his life ten times over.*"

"*Then let it end.*" *She heard the witch's words like a whisper of ice.*

"*How can I let it end, when the price of freedom is more loss? You've taken everything already.*"

The hallway didn't answer.

"*I will not give you my Hounds.*"

The wolf at her side looked up, unused to hearing her speak aloud.

"*You lost them once, and it didn't break you,*" *said the silent castle.*

The Huntress bared her teeth.

"*I don't have time for riddles.*" *She continued pacing, chafing at the pain in her back and the nagging feeling that, after all these years, she was no closer to understanding the curse than she had been when it was cast.*

How could she end something she did not understand? How could she know what she couldn't bear to lose, until she lost it?

It was all madness, like all magic, obeying rules that warped beneath the practitioner's hand, binding itself to the fabric of the world until there was no way to remove it from the weave.

"Tell me this, at least. What does Rowan have to do with this?"

Wind gusted down the hallway, and she could have sworn she heard a hint of laughter in its high, mad sigh.

Chapter Eleven

"Come with me," the Huntress said, standing in the doorway of the library.

I looked up from the book open across my knees. She wore the clothes I had come to associate with her absences: leather hunting breeches; tall, fur-lined boots; leather jerkin; thick wool tunic; and the heavy bearskin cloak. Her hair hung heavy over one shoulder, loosely confined to a dark braid, and her eyes . . . I looked away.

I should never have spoken to her about Avery. Something had changed. Now, when she looked at me, she saw me, and I had the feeling what she saw no longer looked like the shaking, ragged creature she'd dragged in from the cold. Or rather, dragged *into* the cold.

"Come with you where?"

"I want to show you something."

I frowned at her. Her eyes flicked up to my furrowed brow, and the corners of her mouth twitched up in something that might have been a smile.

"You have been in this library for days. Even your wolf pup is bored, and I am tired of resting. Come outside."

I glanced at the shuttered window. Light spilled from the edges of the shutter, falling across the golden eyes of the pup. When had her eyes turned gold? I wondered. She whined softly and left off worrying the frayed edge of the carpet. Besides, it wasn't as if I had found anything in my research. I set the book aside and stood.

The Huntress turned with her usual grace and set off down the stairs. I followed, grabbing my cloak off the back of the chair. The clothes I wore inside and the clothes I wore outside were much the same, since I rarely ventured further than the courtyard, and besides most of them came from the chest at the foot of the bed, which seemed to contain only winter things. Even the red dress was cut from winter-weight wool. I pushed all thoughts of the dress out of my mind. Something about it unsettled me.

It was late afternoon, and the slanting light of the sun cast the mountain in a sheet of gold. The snow sparkled like gleaming steel, and everything had a sharpness to it, clarity like the edge of a knife framing even the shadows. The iron gate had wrought itself anew, the black stark against the white of the snow and the white of the roses, and I slipped past, careful not to let so much as a rusting flake touch my sleeve. Not that the gate showed any sign of rust. Like the rest of the castle, it defied the touch of age.

The pup peeled away from my side, scenting her brothers and sisters, and the Huntress placed a light finger on my shoulder, halting the command in my throat.

"Let her go," she said. "She is a wolf, not a dog, and she needs to be with her own kind."

I wanted to protest. I felt naked without the wolf, but the pack stayed behind. Apparently, wherever we were going did not offer them enough of an incentive to join us. The wind pressed my cloak against me, pushing me after her toward the shore of the lake. There was no sign of the bear, for which I was grateful—not that I would have necessarily seen it against the white of the snow. The wind picked up past the shelter of the walls. It tossed the Huntress's hair around her face, snarling and gnashing as it tore through my furs. I shoved my hands deeper into my clothes and looked up at the walls. Clouds gathered over the lake as the wind shifted the snow in dunes and drifts. I shivered, and broke into a run to keep up with her.

"Here," the Huntress said when we reached the middle. The

surface of the lake felt different under my feet, and the wind grew even stronger. "Here" was nothing, only windswept ice, and a cold so numbing my lips might as well have belonged to a stranger.

I gazed again at the mountains and the peaks above us, and as I watched a beam of sunlight broke through the clouds and fell on the keep's tallest turret. It stained the granite red, a pale hue that tricked the eye with a parody of warmth, breathtaking against the grays and blacks and whites of winter and so untouchable I could have sobbed had the tears not threatened to freeze to my cheeks. I tried to picture what the keep had looked like when banners flew from the turrets and laughter filled the halls and the stables smelled of hay and horse while the torches spilled light out into the winter night. There was beauty there, beyond the ache of solitude. Beside me, the Huntress fell to one knee.

I suppose it is that beautiful, I thought, before I realized she was scraping the snow away from the ice beneath our feet. I thought of the stitches straining against her skin, and a sharp pain of longing shot through me, followed by fear. I remembered the dark green of the vine against her torn flesh, and the sharp pull of the rose in my palm.

"Look."

I knelt beside her and tugged the furs more tightly around my shoulders with my good hand. She scraped the last of the snow free from the ice, and there beneath the surface swam a shoal of fish. For a moment I was back on the wharf, rough wood against the thin cloth of my summer dress, watching the few fish who dared brave the busy waters of the harbor while Sara, or sometimes my father, spoke to the men and women on the ships.

There was something different about these fish. I leaned closer, then gasped. They did not move. They were frozen, round eyes fixed on some distant hope, their scales glittering in the high, clear light of the winter sun.

"Look beneath them."

Sure enough, past the frozen school, partially obscured by the blue-black depths, swam a second shoal. These circled lazily, dark bodies heavy with cold. I looked up to find her watching me. Eyes shouldn't be that green, I thought, momentarily arrested. There was a question there, written somewhere between the bottomless black of iris and curl of eyelash. I opened my mouth to speak, and the wind snatched away both the words and the thoughts that formed them. Kneeling, she looked much younger, more like a girl and less like Winter herself. Kneeling, she was harder to hate, and I watched, transfixed, as a flake of snow melted on her cheek. Was I imagining the sudden flush beneath her skin, or was that just another trick of the light?

"Are they alive?" I asked.

"What do you think?"

I tore my eyes away from her and stared back at the fish. They didn't blink. Then again, I was not sure if fish blinked at all. Their gills remained as stationary as the rest of them while my breath plumed in the air. I wondered how long they had been frozen there, and how long it would take them to thaw.

How long will it take me to thaw?

"Yes," I said, and my heart broke at the shred of hope I saw in her face. This was what came out of a lifetime of frost. Fish, caught at the surface when it froze. Perhaps they had slowed, unaware of the grip of ice until it was too late, blood giving up ground vessel by vessel until scales flowed over solid ice instead of flesh, or perhaps it had been instant. Here, at the center of the lake, with the castle a red gleam behind her, I understood.

The Huntress had not brought me here to show me fish. I was looking at her heart.

The wind picked up again, bringing with it the sounds of pines so much like surf. A beam of sunlight caught the scales of one of the fish, painting it red and blue and green before it vanished, and the brilliance of her world became too much. I couldn't breathe. There were truths here that hurt to look at even out of the corner of my eye, and the agony of a life spent in this place, with its beauty and its emptiness, cut me deeper than thorn or blade.

It was no wonder her heart had frozen.

The sun faded. Clouds wiped the red from the walls of the keep, painting it safely gray again. The wind shrieked a little louder and blew a little colder, and the howl in the back of my throat turned into a cry as the illusion of warmth bled to death on frozen pinnacles of snow. I turned and ran from her, away over the ice toward the distant forest, and the wind lifted my arms like wings. She did not stop me, and I did not look back to see what I had left behind or how much she might have seen in my face.

I was gasping for air by the time the trees began to cast their shadows at my feet, and the tears froze and cracked on my cheeks. I did not know who I wept for: the fish, the Huntress, or myself.

"Why?" I screamed. The sound reverberated around the bowl of the lake, and somewhere a wolf raised his head to howl. Another voice joined it, and another, until every hair on my body had raised in recognition and alarm, but the Huntress did not reply.

I wrapped my furs around me, breathing in the steam from my breath to thaw my face. I was cold. Dangerously cold, with the sweat from my flight drying on my body. I looked up at the sky, still light against the dark of the pines. A snowflake landed on my lashes.

More flakes fell, whirling through the pines and dancing in gusts across the lake. From this distance, the keep looked like something out of a tapestry, woven by a hand whose only experience of cold was what could be glimpsed beyond the warmth of the hearth.

I did not remember sitting, but the snow mounted on my knees, a dim pressure that reminded me of the wolf pup. For a moment, through the fast fall of night, I thought I saw the front door of our little house in the village. It had looked so bleak in the early spring when we first arrived. Our town house had been brightly painted, and the garden full of my mother's roses. This cottage was all hewn timber and thatch. Dead stalks had poked out of a large rectangle in the yard, hinting at the remains of a kitchen garden, and the barn was full of old manure. It was the kind of place a peasant girl might dream of, and my heart ached for a moment as I remembered Sara's parting words.

"What am I supposed to do without you?" I had asked her.

"This would have happened either way," she said. "Do you really think the Duke, or whoever your father decides to marry you off to, would have let his wife run wild with a girl from the stables?"

"Do you think I would have given him a choice?"

Sara had put both hands on my shoulders and looked me in the face. "I forget, sometimes, that knowing how to read and write doesn't make you smart. There are a thousand ways he could have prevented you, many of them legal, some of them not, but no one would have dared question him. At least this way you can still write me letters."

If I could send a letter now, what would I say to her? That I needed her to raise an army to come rescue me? Or would I tell her the truth, the truth that burned colder than the cloud-covered stars, which was that the only thing worse than my captivity was what awaited me on my return?

I thought of my sisters and my father and the little house, a warm light set deep in the mouth of a trap I would spring no matter where I stepped. I belonged to Avery now, and if not Avery, some other man. I looked down at my body, hidden beneath my furs, and hated it. My body was the real prison, something to be bartered or sold or carried away on the back of a great white bear. This was the truth that Sara had tried to tell me, the truth I had not wanted to see, the truth that now was as clear to me as the biting cold.

You could stay here, whispered the part of me that I had never quite been able to silence. *You could stay here with the Huntress and her wolves, and make something new.*

My family already thought me dead, or at least lost forever. They would never need to know that I had chosen this life. I would fade in their memories as my mother had, until the pain of loss became bearable and I passed into mountain myth, the girl who was carried away into the winter night by the Huntress on her great white bear, and in time they would remember how to laugh, as would I. The snow fell harder, and I thought I saw the faces of my sisters rise up out of the white.

"I'll miss you," I told them, my chest constricting at the thought of never seeing them again. They would be happy, though, in the village. Aspen would marry, and Juniper was young enough to find a place for herself, with or without a man.

I would have left them anyway, I realized, tasting the truth of it in the snow. I might have lasted a year, wed to Avery, and then I would have packed a bag in the night and made my way back to the city, or killed him, or fallen in love with the wrong wood-cutter's daughter. I never had a future there that didn't end in grief. Here, at least, the ending was uncertain.

I stood. My legs were numb and moved so slowly they might as well have been unresponsive. My arms were a little better, as I had kept them tucked beneath the furs around my chest, and I beat at my legs in a vain attempt to bring back feeling. When that failed, I crawled toward the shore of the lake, hauling my body through the drifts in slow, painful jerks as my knees remembered their duty.

Past the shelter of the pines, the wind stole whatever warmth I had left, howling with the force and fury of a blizzard, and I realized I had no idea in which direction the castle lay.

No no no no no, my mind chittered. *Not now*. I could not freeze to death, now that I had decided to stay. I flung my arm over my face to shield my eyes from the worst of the storm. I had two choices. I could try my luck crossing the lake in a whiteout, or I could hug the shore, which would eventually bring me to the keep. Assuming, of course, eventually occurred before I froze to death. I tried to visualize the bowl of the crater. The lake had to be at least a mile from shore to shore, but it was longer than it was wide. To go around could take hours, and it was nearly full dark.

I did not have hours, and I would not survive out here at night.

I had to get home.

At the thought, the rose stirred in my blood, nodding like a blossom toward the sun.

There.

In a way, it was a blessing that my legs refused to hold my weight for long. The wind was weaker this close to the ice, and would have knocked me over if I had dared to stand. I moved one limb at a time. Beneath me swam the Huntress's fish, trapped in a murky twilight, fins churning slowly through the black.

The strength of the rose's pull faded as the cold bit deeper and deeper. Strange shapes formed in the gusts, and ice gathered on my lashes, fragmenting my vision. Once, I thought I saw the Huntress astride a white horse, her head thrown back in laughter, a hawk on her wrist. Then the wall of white changed, and she was only snow.

I crawled on.

The snow parted again, and I saw my mother. The memory was piercingly real. She had my thick, wild black hair, and Aspen's lips. I reached for her, but she looked past me, through me, and then she too was gone.

Even the wolves were made of snow. They circled me, howling, only to vanish when I turned my head. I stopped looking and kept my eyelids closed but for a sliver, to protect them from the cold. The howling grew louder and more insistent. "I'm here," I tried to shout, but the words were ripped from my mouth by the wind.

The first time I fell flat on my chest, I struggled back up, my muscles as unpredictable as water. The second time I fell, I managed to roll over and haul myself on my elbows. The third time, I stayed down, and the cruelty of my body's betrayal, now that I had chosen life, bit deeper than the cold.

Where was the Huntress? Where were her hounds, or her roses, or any of the other beasts that roamed her halls?

More faces came and went, fading in and out of the wind. Somewhere my pup was hungry. Somewhere my sisters huddled before a fire, mourning me for dead and clinging to secret hopes. This was the price I would pay for betraying them.

The howl ripped out of my throat with all the anguish of their imagined cries. It was a sound unlike anything I had ever made before, and it ripped my soul loose from its foundation. It went on for a long time, longer than I had breath, and then a hot tongue licked my frozen face, and I realized that the howl was no longer my own but the cry of the she-wolf, her teats heavy, her muzzle lifted to the storm. The rest of the pack materialized out of the snow, even the black wolf little more than a white shadow.

"Rowan."

The roughness of her voice and the feeling of weightlessness as she lifted me in her arms registered on the same level as the swirling snow, and felt only slightly more real. I felt the harsh fur of the bear against my face and lips, and then we were flying, the bear's strides parting the blizzard until the iron gates loomed ahead, and then the smell of roses overwhelmed me.

She had let the girl go.

It had seemed harmless enough to show her the lake's secrets. She had not expected to find pain out there on the ice, and then the storm had risen to meet night and not even the wolves could track Rowan's scent.

Her grip tightened on the still body in her arms. The storms had never hidden something from her before, but this storm had been different. It had fought her, wrestling against the power left to her by the witch, twisting and snarling whenever she tried to grasp it.

"Come back to me," she said into the stiff, frozen hide of Rowan's hood. "Come back to me."

She had seen her future as the winds swept away all evidence that a girl named Rowan had ever lived. Empty hallways, abandoned rooms, roses creeping across the unmarked graves of everyone she had ever cared for, or could have cared for, leaving her alone with her wolves for all eternity.

That might have been enough, once.

"Not yet," she pleaded with gods she'd never believed in. "Please, not yet."

Chapter Twelve

Warmth.

The thought drifted through the dream of spring, echoed in the rush of meltwater. I soaked up the feeling. It had been a while since I'd been warm, because . . . my mind hesitated, as skittish as a wild animal.

Snow. Wolves. The Huntress.

I tried to move. Something heavy lay across my chest. I opened my eyes to a dark room, lit only by the light of the roaring fire. Furs covered all I could see of my body. I was lying on my side, and the weight on my ribs was comforting rather than claustrophobic, as was the smooth, soft warmth behind me. I leaned back into it, my body craving the heat, my mind still drowsy from cold and fatigue.

The warmth moved, too.

Awareness poured into me, mercilessly informing me that my toes and fingers still ached with frostbite, and also that I was very, very naked. The body beside me, that wondrous source of warmth, was also naked, and there was only one person on this mountain to whom that body could belong.

"Skin to skin. It is the only way to save someone as cold as you are."

I froze as her words drifted across my ear. Something moved at my feet, and I saw the tip of a white ear. The wolves were here, too. *My pack.* Leaves rustled just outside the edge of hearing, and

I tried to sit up, but her arm weighed a thousand pounds and my muscles refused to obey me. There was a strange clacking sound, like old bones knocking together, and as she pulled me closer, I realized the sound was my teeth chattering.

"You are safe. I promise."

Her body was as soft and hard as she was. I could feel the muscles of her stomach move as she spoke, and the curve of her breasts pressed against my back. She was wrong. I was not safe. In fact, I had never been more in danger. I remembered the decision I had come to in the snow. My heart beat faster, stuttering in my chest.

"Breathe slowly," she said. "Cold can weaken the heart."

I closed my eyes against the bitter irony of her words. My heart stuttered again, then resumed its beat, and I took a deep breath of warm air. The breath brought me closer to her, and the torpor that clung to my limbs prevented me from rolling away from the heat of her skin and the cool, piney scent of her hair. I shuddered as she held me while the nearness of my death passed over me like a winged shadow, and the feel of her arm around me was all that kept the ice at bay.

"It will pass."

"The storm came out of nowhere," I said, grateful that she could not see my face.

"Rowan." She pulled away from me, leaving me once again out in the snow, and I shivered uncontrollably as she propped herself up on one elbow to look into my eyes. I saw the accusation there.

"I didn't," I said, my body shaking uncontrollably. "I didn't want to die."

"You didn't?"

I wanted to touch her then, but all I could do was lie there while the last of the cold left me in great, shuddering tremors.

"No."

"Then why did you run?"

Hold me, my mind screamed. "It's all I know how to do," said my mouth.

117

"You should not have stopped running."

I closed my eyes against her words, hurt seeping in around the cold.

"If you had kept running, you would not have frozen."

"If I had kept running, you would not have found me."

"Open your eyes, Rowan."

I refused. If I opened my eyes, I would see her skin, glowing rose-gold in the firelight as light spilled over her shoulders and breasts and the little pool of shadow between her collarbones, and she would see everything.

"I'm cold," I said, hoping she mistook the shaking in my voice for a different kind of need.

"Here." She lay back down beside me, pulling me against her.

I continued to shake, but this time with the effort of keeping my heart inside my body. She ran her hand down my arm the way I had seen her stroke a wolf, or the bear, and I bit my lip against the longing that followed her touch.

I am sick with cold, I tried to tell myself. *I did not come back for this. I came here to escape Avery.*

The denial lasted all of another heartbeat as I lay, trembling, seeing stars behind my eyes and hearing the quick draw of my breath as she swept her fingers over the curve of my shoulder and down to my wrist, then up, careless, unaware of the desire spreading from her fingertips like fire.

I wanted to turn, to feel her hands on the tips of my breasts, on my lips, on the smooth skin of my stomach and the hard line of my collarbones, but I didn't dare with my heart so close to hers and winter still gripping my marrow. I lay there until the last shudder of desire faded, and the world went soft around the edges as warmth, real and lasting, flooded me like wine.

"Tell me about the roses," I said from the center of this new, warm world.

"You've never heard the story of the Winter Rose?"

"No."

A wolf rose, stretched, then flopped back down on the floor.

"Would you like to hear it?"

"Yes," I said, remembering with a twinge that was almost bittersweet the contempt I'd felt for Avery's stories.

"In the mountains, we believe that the Earth was born in Winter. Everything was cold and dark, and the sun only rose for a few hours each day, too weak to manage much else. Winter might have been beautiful then, and she might have been cruel, but there was no one there to see or feel, and so instead she was just lonely. She watched the Sun coming and going and asked him one day why he didn't stay.

"'There is nothing for me here,' he said to her. And so Winter thought long and hard about what she might do to keep him in her skies. First, she made the North Wind. She was a powerful thing, and for a time her company was all that Winter wanted. Eventually, however, she remembered why she had breathed the North Wind into life, and so she sent her daughter on a journey far across the world, to see if there was anything that caught the Sun's attention. The North Wind was gone a long time, and Winter began to worry until her daughter returned one day just after sunset.

"'I have watched the sun for a year,' she said to her mother, 'and nothing pleases him.'

"This grieved Winter, and Winter's grief cut the North Wind to the quick, for she loved her mother.

"'The Sun is warm,' she said at last, trying to cheer her mother up. 'And you are cold. Perhaps if you make something warm, the Sun will stay.'

"Winter thought about this, and at last saw the wisdom in her daughter's words, and so she created the South Wind. The longer the South Wind blew, the longer the Sun stayed in her sky, and Winter rejoiced, for the Sun loved her and she loved him. Together, they made Summer, and life bloomed across the world.

"But as life grew, Winter faded, and at last she realized the terrible truth. The Sun's love burned too hot, and if she stayed with him, she would die. So, Winter made a pact with the Sun. For the sake of their child, they would part, and Sun would visit Winter for only a short time each year. The children Winter bore in these times were Spring and Fall, and Winter loved them, but she was not happy, for the time passed too quickly and she never saw Summer again.

"The North Wind stayed with her, for she was Winter's first daughter, and the most loyal, but her mother's sorrow made her bitter and cruel. One day, tired of grief, she blew into the heart of Summer and plucked a rose from her bosom to bring back to their mother. The rose should have died, but the strength of the North Wind's conviction froze death, and so it bloomed, spreading across the ice, Winter's only living memory of her lost child.

"Now, a northern woman who is beautiful and unattainable is called a Winter Rose," the Huntress finished, "and mothers who have lost children leave carved figurines where the winter roses grow in midwinter, sharing their grief with the season."

I looked up. Her hair fell around her face, but the firelight shone through, and the shadows it cast were dark and wild.

"Is that why the roses follow you?"

"No," she said, and the bitter smile that twisted her lips told a story that I was no longer sure I wanted to hear. "You should sleep, Rowan."

"Wait," I said, fighting to keep my eyes open. I had decided to stay here, out in the snows, with a woman who I knew so little about, it wouldn't have filled a half page of one of her books. "Tell me your name."

I had almost given up on the question by the time she replied.

"Names have power, Rowan. Not power like this," she touched my bandaged hand, "but still, power. What is your name to you?"

"My name? It's just a name, I guess. Who I am."

"Your mother named you Rowan?"

"Yes."

"And your sisters, Aspen and Juniper. We call those trees the mountain sisters."

"I know."

"Your friends in the city by the sea called you Rowan."

"Yes."

"All of that is a part of your name." She paused. "The woman

I was, before. I don't want to remember her. Or the people she lost."

"And her name would be a memory," I said.

"Yes."

I burrowed deeper under the furs, struggling to decide how much to say. "I understand, I think," I said at last. "There have been plenty of times these past few years where I would have given anything to be someone else. When my mother died, or when we had to flee the city, and especially when I realized that my father planned to wed me to some boorish villager who didn't know one end of an abacus from another. It's funny now, that that seems like the worst of it all."

"A marriage is a lifetime."

"My father was going to trade me. I was the price of our new life, of his stupid furs, of the house that *I* found at the bottom of my mother's inheritance, and it didn't matter what I wanted. I told Aspen and Juniper that it would be okay there. I promised them we would be happy, and then we got there and they fit in, and it was only I who hated everyone. I tried. Or maybe I didn't. I don't know. It all seems so stupid now."

Something warm and furry clambered over the furs and pounced on my face. A hot, wet tongue bathed my eyelids, and I struggled to free my ear from needle-sharp teeth as the pup whined her enthusiasm for my return.

"I let a boy die once before I became the Huntress, simply because he irritated me. Everything is relative."

I couldn't quite bring myself to look at the Huntress. The pup licked my nose with an impossibly long tongue, then flopped down on my chest to chew a spot on her leg, apparently content once more with her world.

"How did he die?"

"I took him on a hunt. He was green, and the hounds found a bear."

I flinched at the thought of the wounds on her back. I did not want to talk about death. "How are you healing?"

She sat, turning so that I could see her shoulder. Her skin had

121

knitted over the gashes, and beneath the translucent flesh the rose still grew, green and black and white, like some sort of queer tattoo. I raised a hand to touch it, but the pup pounced at the movement, wrestling my wrist back down to my chest and growling fiercely.

"Let's take a look at that hand before she chews it off." The Huntress peeled off the bandage, and I looked away, not wanting to see the damage or what lay beneath the cuts. "There are advantages to magic, if you can learn to live with it," she said.

I looked.

A rose bloomed at the center of my palm, but unlike the roses on the walls, this one was blood red, and the skin around it was almost totally healed. I touched it tentatively. Skin, not petals, met my fingertips, but I heard the rustle of leaves.

"It's beautiful," I said, because it was, no matter what else it meant, no matter what else it would bring with it. I held it up to the light, transfixed. When the pup lunged again, I batted her away without pain.

"Your pup is growing," said the Huntress.

"Yes."

"She'll be ready for her first hunt soon."

I looked from the red rose to the gold of the pup's eyes in her black face, and wondered at the strangeness of it all. "You said she should have died."

"She would have, without you."

"You said she would only breed more suffering."

"She might. Or she might not."

I smoothed the fur on the pup's face, thinking of bears and elk and all the dangers of the wild that she would face as she grew. I would be helpless to save her, then. "I am not a green boy," I said, an idea forming in my mind. "Take me with you, next time you hunt."

She placed a hand on my cheek, turning my face toward her, and searched my eyes for a long time. I did not know what she saw, or what, indeed, she was looking for, but when she let me go she nodded.

Outside, a wolf lifted its muzzle to howl.

She lay with the girl in her arms long into the cold, dark blue of the night. Past the roof, if she closed her eyes, she could see the stars: the Hunter with his bow striding across the heavens, the Great Bear foraging along the crest of the mountain, and the Wolf prowling the horizon. They looked down at her out of glittering eyes.

She knew what they saw.

In the violet sprawl of the heavens, she felt the earth shift beneath her, the ice thinning, a hint of thaw breaking free from the snow to blow over the lake, redolent with long-dead leaves and moss.

She wanted to run.

She wanted to stay.

She wanted to hold this girl like this forever, winter stretching into eternity in a long breath of frost while Rowan's dark hair brushed the Huntress's cheek.

"Freedom will bring you no joy," the witch had said.

She did not want freedom.

This was enough, this small moment, this brief promise of respite from an ache she had not thought to name till now.

I will teach you to hunt, *she told Rowan in the quiet of her mind.* I will show you the beauty of my wilds, the glory of the heights, and then you will not leave me.

Chapter Thirteen

The Huntress led me down a spiral staircase near the stables, holding a torch.

"Are you taking me to your dungeon?" I asked, only half joking. I hadn't explored this part of the keep for a reason, I didn't want to encounter anything large and hairy that might dwell here.

"Not quite. In here." She opened an iron-bound door into a room that smelled of steel and leather. My jaw dropped when she held the torch aloft. The room was ringed with rack after rack of weapons: swords, shields, bows, arrows, spears, axes, knives, and other things I didn't have a name for.

"You could raze a village with this," I said in a hushed voice.

"We did."

She walked to the far side of the room and ran her hand across a row of spears, selecting a tall, narrow-shafted length of bright-tipped ash and tossing it to me. I caught it. The wood felt strange beneath my fingers, more like metal or bone than branch.

"You need a spear for larger game. An arrow will only irritate a bear or boar unless you get it in the eye, and you can defend yourself against almost anything you'll find out there with the shaft. Come here."

I obeyed, stopping before the wall of bows. The Huntress selected a few, measuring them against my height with a critical eye before selecting a smaller bow made of some sort of dark polished wood.

"You don't need a longbow, and it would take months, maybe years, of work before you could draw it. This is a hunter's bow. It will bring down a deer or a rabbit easily enough, and it won't take up as much room when you're not using it."

The bow's grip felt strangely comforting in my hand. The only weapon I had ever handled was my father's sword, and never with his permission. My father drew the line at arming his daughters, and my mother hadn't lived long enough to argue the matter. *She would have known how to shoot*, I realized, tracing the leather of the grip with my thumb. Any mountain girl knew how to kill and skin a rabbit. That was considered a useful skill, unlike reading, as Avery had been quick to point out. I tightened my hold.

The Huntress found me a quiver, bowstring, archer's glove and guard, and a whetstone before leading me back to the surface. I tried not to trip over the spear on the steps, but the butt clanged a few times, emphasizing just how much more quietly the Huntress moved than I did. I watched her boots in the spaces between clangs.

Something was different.

No.

Everything was different.

I had awakened to find her gone, with only the wolf pup keeping me company. Her chambers were larger than mine, but not as large as some of the abandoned rooms of state I'd wandered through on the days I'd spent alone here. She made her bed in a sea of furs, and the usual hunting tapestries hung on the walls, but the room still had the feel of a servant's quarters despite its size. It was only as I was leaving, dressed in the clean, dry clothes she'd laid beside the bed for me that I realized where I was. This was the room above the stables, where the master of horse might have lived, or the mistress of the hunt. It provided easy access to the stalls below and overlooked the courtyard, giving the occupant a full view of the castle's comings and goings, but it was not the sort of room a chieftain's daughter might have lived in. The more I thought I learned about the Huntress, the less I knew.

She had not spoken of my brush with death again. I'd wandered down to the kitchen, my heart lodged too fully in my throat to eat, only to find her waiting in her hunting leathers. Neither of us acknowledged the tenderness she'd shown me the night before.

"Put these on," she told me now in the courtyard, handing me the gloves and guard. "We'll start with the bow."

I tugged the arm guard on over my wool shirt and fumbled with the glove. It was in need of oiling, but fit relatively well once I got it on. I watched the Huntress out of the corner of my eye as she hauled an old target made of sacking and aged straw out of the bowels of the stable, trying not to remember the feel of her skin against mine.

"Any idea how to string a bow?" she asked me when she returned.

"You put the loop over the end."

"Try it."

I secured the string to the nock on the lower limb of the bow and tried to bend it.

"Stop." She put a hand on my shoulder. "Brace the bow against your boot, or it will slip."

I tried again. It was hard to concentrate with her standing so close to me, but I managed to bend the bow enough to slip the bowstring into place.

"Good. Here."

I took the arrow she offered and nocked it, preparing to draw.

"There are two ways to shoot a bow," she said, moving her hand down my arm to adjust my grip. "The proper way, and the necessary way. We'll start with the proper way."

She raised my elbow as she spoke, then turned my body perpendicular to the target.

"Widen your stance," she said, and there was no way to convince myself I was not acutely aware of how little space separated her lips from my ear. I moved my foot back, which brought me up against her body.

"What's the necessary way?" I asked, to keep myself from thinking.

"The way you'll shoot in the woods. Pull back with your first two fingers and sight down the shaft toward the target. When you're ready, release."

She stepped away from me, and I let out a breath I hadn't realized I'd been holding. The target seemed very far away from the tip of the arrow and my arm shook with the effort of the draw. I missed.

"Now watch me." The Huntress plucked the bow from my hand. She nocked and released before I could blink, the arrow hitting the target with a thunk. Then she shot again, and again, standing, kneeling, and once, lying in the snow. Each time, the arrow found its mark, and when she turned to me at last I recognized the gleam in her eye for what it was: joy.

"Now, watch as I do it the proper way." This time, she stood as I had, with her feet squared beneath her shoulders. She released three arrows in quick succession, then slowed for my benefit. "Do you see?"

"I think so."

"You learn how to walk before you run, but you won't always have time in the woods to perfect your stance. Or the space." She handed the bow back to me.

"How long did it take you to shoot like that?"

"I learned to ride a horse before I could walk, and my mother gave me the hilt of her dagger to teethe on. I was born to the hunt, Rowan. Do not compare yourself to me. Try again. This time, breathe through it, and find the target with your eye as well as the arrow. Your body knows what to do."

I am not sure I trust my body, I thought as she adjusted my stance again, the length of her leg touching mine. What would she think if she could see my thoughts?

I bit my lip and released. This arrow was closer than the first, and I tried to concentrate on that instead of the dull ache of anxiety that had taken root in my bones. What I felt for the Huntress seemed natural enough to me, but this was not the city, where women could live together without judgement unless, of course, they were the daughters of wealthy merchants with dowries the size of ships. I was also mortal. Whatever the Huntress was, however human she had felt beside me, there was something in her that was too wild to be mere flesh and blood and bone.

I had heard the stories told by sailors about women possessed of unearthly beauty who sang to passing ships from rocky shoals, luring captains to their deaths, and mermaids who seduced men before they drowned them. Henrik had even told us stories about women farther north who wore the skins of seals. If a man stole their skin while they were bathing, he said, the women would be trapped on land forever. Every seafaring culture had stories about dangerously beautiful women, and in each the lesson was clear: beauty killed you.

What stories, I wondered, did they tell about the Huntress?

"Feel the arrow here, and here, and here." She touched my hand, my shoulder, and my stomach, encircling my waist with her arm. "Breathe," she said, and I did, feeling the pressure of her hand.

"Draw."

I pulled back the arrow, and she guided my wrist with her other hand, her arm resting against mine.

"Aim."

Her hair brushed against my cheek as she sighted with me down the shaft. I narrowed my eyes, focusing until the target filled my vision and my heartbeat matched that of the Huntress.

"Now."

I released. The arrow took the target in the left-hand corner, and pride overrode desire as I turned to her for approval, not bothering to hide the smile on my face. She squeezed my waist, pulling me to her with some of the same fierce joy I'd seen in her face earlier.

"Well done, Rowan," she said into my ear, and I decided this must be how eagles felt, soaring over the peaks, higher than any other living thing on earth.

I hit the target what felt like a hundred more times that morning before she took the bow out of my hand.

"How do you feel?"

I swore there was a glint of sadism in her eyes. "Like my arms are made of dough," I said, letting the arms in question hang limply at my sides. The only benefit of my shaking muscles was that there was no room left for other earthly wants.

"You'll be wishing they felt like dough tomorrow. Come, some wine will help."

I walked beside her on the way back to the kitchen, carrying my bow and spear. There was something unsettlingly right about walking into her hall armed to the teeth, even if I didn't have a clue what to do with one of the weapons in my hands, and was too weak from learning how to use the other to so much as pluck the string.

This was how I used to feel reading epic poems about long-dead warriors, or listening to Henric tell stories about his people's warrior gods and goddesses. Limitless. I widened my stride, letting a little more of the yoke of the past few years slide off me.

Beside me, the Huntress smiled.

"You were wasted on your village boy," she said, and I felt the weight of the arm she did not place around my shoulder like a ghostly caress.

"Thank you," I said, feeling my chin tilt a little higher and not caring that I might look ridiculous, strutting into the warmth of the kitchen.

"Put up your bow and heat us some wine. I have something else for you," she said, and this time I did feel the slight pressure of her hand on my back.

The pup tried to wrest the spear from me when I leaned it against the wall. "Stop that," I scolded her, smiling despite myself. The smile stayed on my lips as I heated the wine, and it was still there when the Huntress returned. She paused in the doorway, her eyes widening a little as they met mine, and then I saw the object in her hands.

It was fur, but not just any fur.

"You'll need this in the snow," she said, settling the wolfskin cloak around my shoulders. I stroked the white ruff, feeling the power of the departed animal rippling through the flawlessly tanned hide like a subvocal growl.

129

"Was this . . . was this one of yours?" I asked her in a hushed voice. She smoothed the cloak, pulling it more securely around me, and I saw the answer in her face. "But you said they were your family."

"They are."

I had nothing to say to that. The blood rose to my face, and I stood there with her hands on my shoulders and the wolf's pelt soft beneath my hands, unable to breathe at the magnitude of what had been left unsaid.

"I . . ." I managed at last, stumbling over my words. "No one has ever given me anything like this. Ever."

"I thought you were a wealthy merchant's daughter."

I touched her hand, and what she saw in my face made her turn away from me, reaching for the wine. "Thank you," I added, somewhat lamely. She placed a horn of wine in my hand, then reached behind me and lifted the hood over my head.

"There."

I reached up and felt the ridge of snout and curve of ears. The heaviness in the air between us lessened, and I tilted my head as I had seen her wolves do. She surprised me with a laugh, and then she did wrap her arm around my shoulders, pulling me close enough to whisper. I heard her words, muffled though they were by the hood.

"It suits you too well, Rowan."

Rowan's smile split the gray morning.

The Huntress crouched, readying herself for another lunge as the girl adjusted her grip on the spear. The Huntress had wrapped the spearhead at Rowan's insistence, for all that the girl had yet to land a blow, but her last thrust had been close.

I've missed this.

She'd had too many thoughts like that, of late. The space between her worlds was shrinking, and Rowan stood at the center of that divide, her dark curls blowing in the snow.

"Strike. Pretend I am a bear."

Rowan struck, and the Huntress stopped the point with her hand, letting it rest against her ribs.

"Well struck."

Rowan pulled away, feinted, and struck again, and this time the Huntress was glad she'd wrapped the spear because it caught her underneath her left breast with a sharpness that took her breath away.

"Are you hurt?"

Rowan was at her side in an instant, and any resemblance between this moment and a moment from her past life vanished. None of her Hounds would have fallen to their knees in the snow beside her during a sparring match.

She stood up, brushing snow off the knee that had borne the brunt of her misstep, and raised the girl up with her.

"I am not hurt, because I am not a bear," she said, touching a gloved hand to the girl's cheek. "But if I were a bear I might be dead."

The girl's cheek flushed where her glove touched her, and something in the Huntress stirred. She could feel the girl's pulse as her glove trailed down her throat, racing, insistent, and the part of the Huntress that had not remembered it was human wanted nothing more than to push Rowan down into the snow and nip at her throat, tangling that dark hair in her hands.

The part of her that was human wanted that, too.

The pressure of the spear brought her back, her own ragged breathing driving the point in closer, and her heartbeat thundered down the shaft and deep into the mountain, echoing down the slopes in warning and in need. She pulled away.

"Tomorrow."

"Tomorrow what?" Rowan called after her, and she heard the frustration in the girl's voice.

"We hunt."

Chapter Fourteen

The day of my first hunt dawned with a howl. The shutters on my window clattered, straining at the hinges, and I pulled the thick curtains more tightly over them to stop the draft. Even the fire in my little hearth sputtered, the draw from the blizzard outside sending a shower of sparks upward.

Disappointment came in with the cold. There was no way the Huntress would go out in this, and I did not bother hiding my unhappiness.

"Damn it," I swore, kicking the chest at the foot of the bed and earning myself a sore toe. I could not spend another day in the yard shooting arrows or dancing around the Huntress with a spear. I had calluses on my hands now from weeks of practice, and an ache that followed me around wherever I went, sharpening into a need so deep it felt like pain whenever my eyes fell on the Huntress. The only thing worse than being near her was being away from her. I paced the library or, worse, I tried to read, and my eyes glossed over the words and gleaned no meaning from the letters. A hunt was exactly what I needed. Time spent outside these walls, without the whispering presence of the roses, would clear the air.

None of that seemed likely now. I dressed in my hunting clothes anyway and descended the stairs in search of breakfast, if not for myself, then for the pup, who bumped me playfully with her shoulder.

"When did you get so big?" I asked her, momentarily distracted by the revelation that my runty wolf now reached my hip.

She chose not to answer, and instead chased the drifts that blew in through the arrow slits in the outer hallways, darting from one pile of snow to the next with an enthusiasm I did not share. I followed her, nudging her out of my way now and then when she showed signs of wanting to bite at my boots.

The Huntress was not in the kitchen, but I found my spear propped against the table. Behind it lay a slice of thick brown bread and cheese. I shoved it into my mouth and chewed as quickly as I could, my heart pounding. My heart pounded more often than not these days, and I closed my eyes against the sound before it drove me mad. I tried to concentrate on eating, then gave up, wrapped the rest of the bread in a bit of cloth, shoved it into a pocket, grabbed the spear, and sprinted for the stables.

She was waiting, framed against the blowing snow and wrapped in the huge white bearskin that she'd worn when I first met her. The wolf pack ranged around her, tussling over bits of bone and growling in high spirits. I stood mutely before her and pointed at the snow.

"It's hunting weather," she said, giving me a grin that set off my reckless heart again.

"You're going out in this? You can't see or hear anything," I said, pushing aside the desire to pound my hands against the walls. "Can they even catch a scent in that?" The memory of the storm that had nearly killed me shivered through me. Beyond the stable door the blizzard raged, blowing heavy drifts down the stone aisle. The Huntress paused and tilted her head like a wild thing, as if whatever she had heard had answered her unspoken question.

"Are you not coming then?" she asked.

I pulled my hood up over my head and made to stride past her out of the stable. A huge white shape eclipsed the dim light, lumbering in with an overpowering odor of bear. I took a quick step backward, still not quite used to how easily the large animal moved, and the Huntress caught me around the waist. It was so easy to lean into her. It would be so easy to tilt my face to hers or turn in her arms, the memory of her body in the firelight glowing white-hot.

"Easy," she said, giving me a quick squeeze before she leapt astride the bear, spear in hand.

I stared up at them, awed anew despite myself by the sight of the massive muzzle weaving slowly back and forth, and by the tumble of dark hair pouring from beneath the hood of her cloak. The wolves lifted their heads to howl. The sound echoed in the stable, and I found myself clutching at the pup's fur.

"Rowan," the Huntress said, holding out her hand.

I let her haul me up before her. The motion brought a flash of memory, taking me back to that first ride, and I shoved aside thoughts of my family. She raised her silver hunting horn to her lips and blew, the bugle joining the howls of the wolves, and the pack surged forward, lean, loping shapes vanishing into the teeth of the blizzard, my pup lost somewhere in their midst. Their howls vanished in the greater howl of the storm, and I was grateful for the fur-lined hood of my cloak. A long strand of her hair tangled with my own, blown forward with the shrieking wind. I watched them dance for a moment, black and brown, and then the castle walls loomed out of the white and the dark green of the rose vines sliced through the snow-blasted stone.

Past the gate, whirlwinds of snow tore across the lake, and I leaned back and turned my head against the Huntress's shoulder as one ripped into us. She wrapped her free arm around me and urged the bear into a faster gait while I gave up trying to ignore the feel of her hips and let the cold wind cool my face.

The wolves led us down the slopes to the tree line, where bearded pines and twisted firs clawed for purchase, their boughs too laden with snow for even the blizzard to stir. One of the wolves snapped at a passing hare but he did not give chase, and we rode like we were a part of the storm. The cold did not touch me this time as it had before. I tightened my grip on the Huntress's arm, and if she noticed, she said nothing, just as she

135

never spoke when she caught me watching her from across a room or brushed me aside when I stood too close.

The high, sparse slopes bled into rugged forest, thick with evergreens and a bumper crop of boulders half buried in snow save for where the wind had sheared the drifts, exposing frozen lichen and black rock. I tried to picture my father here, following the Lockland clan deeper and deeper into the heart of the mountains. I could not reconcile the man I knew with this untamed place, so far away from the sea. I thought of the ships in his office, encased in glass bottles, each a model of one of his vessels. He had smashed them, one by one, when they sank. I remembered coming across the splintered wood, lost in the shards of broken bottles, the glass as green as the sea and just as cruel. The trees here were tall enough for masts, if any man dared fell them so far from the coast. The Huntress shifted behind me, and I found I did not want to think of my father.

We rode for hours, or maybe it was only minutes. It could have been a year, for all I knew, tree after tree whipping past us through the storm. Somewhere out there was the boundary. I could feel it past the curtains of snow, an invisible pressure against my temples, different from the pressure building within me.

It was as if my very thought had conjured them. The hedge rose before us in a frozen tangle, taller than a man, taller even than the Huntress atop the bear. Snow piled up on the vines, but the thorns broke free, long, vicious things that put the bloom my father had brought me to shame. Against the thorns, the roses looked fragile, almost delicate, their petals somehow whiter than the snow, or perhaps the palest shade of pink. I tore my eyes away, sure I could hear them whispering.

A rose for a rose, a thorn for a thorn.

It seemed a lifetime ago that those words had grieved me.

The wolves slowed, picking up a scent, and veered away from the lingering presence of the briars and back toward the mountains. I strained my half-closed eyes and muffled ears for sight or sound of what we chased, but all was lost in white.

When the Huntress's breath caught in her throat, mine followed. There, behind a veil of snow, stood a massive bull elk. His back was to a fall of rock, and lichen hung from his massive antlers like tattered velvet. Frost blended with the white hair beneath his chin, and when he snorted a warning at the boldest of the wolves, his breath steamed in the air.

The only elk I had seen this close had been dead, and I was not prepared for its beauty. He was full of life, eyes luminous and muscles hard as he faced the death written in the golden eyes of the wolves.

"Look closely," she whispered into the fur of my hood as she leveled the tip of her spear to point.

The animal's front right leg hung limply, the foreleg swollen and red with frozen blood. He could barely put any weight on it at all, I saw, even when he had to steady himself as a wolf darted in to nip at his heels. I understood, all at once, the brutal compassion in the wolves' hunger, and the mercy in the Huntress's spear.

She slid down from the bear's back without a word, her heavy bearskin cloak nearly vanishing against the snow. Her spear rose taller than she stood. I stared at the tip, stilled by the realization that I was alone on top of the bear. The animal shifted, and once the first bite of fear lost its sting, I let myself feel, for a moment, the power of its muscles ripple through me. *This is how the gods must feel,* I thought, the snowbound forest far below me. I was convinced that, if I wanted to, I could reach out and peel back the white of the sky to reveal the moon. A gust of wind blew the thought away, bringing cold back with it, and I missed the heat of her body.

She circled with the wolves, patient and deadly with her long spear and loose hair. The wind tugged at it with an almost passionate intensity as though nothing pleased it more than running through the tangled locks. I stifled a pang of jealousy. When she struck, a part of me struck with her, staring up into the lowered horns as her spear took the elk in the chest. He sank to his knees, bellowing, and a wolf leapt for his throat. I saw black fur arrested in motion, and hot blood spurting out to continue the arc of his leap, only to end in a red mist across the snow. It was not my pup. Not yet, but I sensed her on the outskirts of the hunt, watching.

The Huntress retrieved the spear when the beast lay still, wiping his heart's blood on the thick fur of his hide. It left a red stain against the brown. She met my eyes as she straightened, a flash of forest green that brought the rest of the woods into sharper clarity before she pulled out a long knife and began sawing off a haunch.

I had seen things killed before. A horse once that had broken its leg in the street, and more chickens than I could count. This was different. Those animals had not fought. They had trusted until their last breath, and sometimes chickens farther down the line had pecked at the blood and feathers of the fallen, oblivious to the fact that they too would soon share that fate. The elk had fought as if he planned on living, even though his death warrant had been signed the moment the wolves scented him. It was a curious thought. Had the Locklands known they were going to die when they saw the Huntress emerge out of the snow? Had that knowledge changed anything?

"You'll want to get down," she said.

I slid off, and she caught me, minimizing the impact of my frozen feet on the ground. I would have objected to her help had the bear been a horse and the Huntress been anyone else, but pride seemed silly somehow out here in the cold. The bear roared the moment I slid free, scattering the wolves, and I flinched as she tore into the carcass, shaking it as if it weighed no more than a kitten.

"It will be easier to let them feed here than to haul it all the way back to the keep," the Huntress said, wrapping the haunch she'd cut free in a length of oilcloth. "And when they are done, the ravens and the foxes will feed, and I will have fewer bones to trip over in the stable."

I listened, unable to wrench my eyes away from the visceral ripping and tearing before us. A few of the braver wolves darted in to snap up the scraps.

"They are not dogs," I said at last, repeating back to her something she had said to me about the pup.

"No."

"How did they come to be yours?"

"They are not mine." She uncorked a flask of water and took a long swig, then passed it to me.

"Then why do they follow you?"

"Why do ravens follow wolves?" she asked, pointing up at the clearing sky. The blizzard was fading, and in place of swirling flakes a flock of birds cawed overhead, circling impatiently. "Wolves provide meat. So do I. They follow me because we hunt better together, and because once, a long time ago . . ." she trailed off and I caught sight of the black wolf. He was watching us, head lowered over the carcass, his eyes a burning yellow that saw right through me. She didn't finish her sentence, and I didn't press her.

A drop of blood on her cheek caught my eye. I fought an overwhelming desire to wipe it away as I looked up into her face. The blizzard blew itself out in a last gust, and pale winter sunlight filtered through the pines, lighting up the flakes of snow in her hair. A savage longing cut through me, sharper than the touch of thorns, and I felt the last shreds of doubt vanish beneath the sound of the feeding wolves. I thought of the little cottage at the end of the lane where my father and sisters huddled against the cold, and of the city house, stripped of its furnishings by the banks. I thought, absurdly, of Henrik, rowing us out to my father's ships to peer up at the decks, the surf breaking against the comforting bulk of their hulls.

All that was gone now. What was more, it had never been mine in the first place. Not the ship, not the town house, not even the cottage where my mother had been born. All that I had ever owned of value was my body, and even that had not been mine to give, so long as I remained in my father's world.

I took a step toward the Huntress, touching the horn at her side with one mittened hand. If she refused me, I would wander off into the snow and lie down in the drifts, empty of purpose, full of broken promise, but free. I had nothing more to lose.

"Rowan," she said, her breath frosting as it passed her lips.

I tugged the mitten off of my hand and raised it to her face, brushing back a lock of hair. It was cold and smooth as it fell against my wrist, and she held very still as my fingers brushed her cheek. A flake of snow melted on her lower lip.

I kissed her, gently at first, the barest touch of my lips against hers, but when her lips parted under mine a roaring filled my ears, and it was all I could do to stand as the axis of the world shifted beneath me. She tasted like pine and snow and the sweet, sharp bite of winter apples. She moved then, her hands pulling me closer and her lips flushing the cold out from underneath my skin, while the pack fed at our backs and somewhere deep inside me the rose put out more roots, tightening its grip around my heart.

Three wolves ran in a line along the hills, threading in and out of trees and memory while snow filled their prints and an owl hooted somewhere in the forest, setting out on silent wings.

Isolde.

The name followed the wolves, and the Huntress caught it, fluttering against the bars of her fingers like a moth, or some small brown bird. The bird spoke her name with the witch's voice, and with that voice came fear.

"For your pride, you may keep your castle and your forests, but only beasts will roam your halls, and all those you love will turn to tooth and claw and cloven hoof, save you. You shall be just as you are, colder than a winter star and just as lovely, and you shall live among them, a huntress, a queen among the bones, until the day comes when you learn what it is like to love helplessly, hopelessly, and truly. Only then will you be free, but freedom will bring you no joy, because the price of freedom will be the loss of one you cannot bear to lose.

"Until then, I will bind you and yours with ice and thorn, until the years have stripped the memory of warmth from your bones and the only thing that blooms around you is the winter rose. As long as those roses grow wild, you shall reign over winter and all her beasts, but beware: where the winter rose takes root, it grows, and its blossoming will mark the end of everything that you now hold dear."

Rowan.

She saw the symmetry of the trap, the way it had sunk into her flesh each time she'd touched the girl, how it had closed so slowly she had not felt the steel beneath soft skin.

She saw a rose on a bloodstained breast and blue eyes wide with an understanding that was blissfully cut short by death.
Helplessly.
Hopelessly.
Truly.
She was going to lose her.

Chapter Fifteen

I pulled the red dress from the chest with shaking hands and laid it on the bed, my hair still steaming from the baths. *You will not run from me,* I thought, stroking the dark wool. *You will not run.*

But she had.

We had ridden back to the keep, and I had laughed in her arms as she pointed out the smaller details of her forests: prints there, a tuft of hair here, water flowing deep beneath the drifts.

I lost her when we passed beneath the shadow of the roses. I felt her stiffen, and I knew before I turned to look that she wore her other face: cold, implacable, inhuman. She helped me off the bear with hands of stone, and I walked away from her, the thrill of the hunt fading into sore muscles while she checked over the wolves for injuries. I fled to a place where she would not hear my heart breaking.

"She kissed me," I told the dress. *She kissed me, and she felt the world tilt, too.*

I stared into the brass mirror I'd found in one of the empty rooms. My eyes were no longer bloodshot, and my hair, clean and combed to the best of my ability, curled in the heat from my fire. I remembered something my sister had said in the months before I left.

"Wear the red dress, Rowan."

I had let her lace it up, hating the game, but there was nothing playful in her face when I'd turned to grumble at her. *"What?"*

"Trust me on this, Row. If you ever decide you do want Avery, or any other man for that matter, wear red. It's . . . it's your color."

"Aspen," I said to the empty room, "you'll laugh, but I need you now."

I slid into the dress. The wool was so finely woven it felt more like linen, and I laced it up as best I could with trembling fingers. The bodice was lower than anything I'd ever worn, though still modest by city standards, showing only the barest hint of cleavage, and it fitted my hips as if it had been made for me. I opened my palm and watched the rose petals ripple in some unseen breeze, wondering if by some fae trick it *had* been made for me, just as my room was always clean and there was always wood stacked against the hearth.

Beneath the dress I had found a pair of simple shoes, and these too fit, the leather supple and soft. I had nothing to put on my face, and I had lost all my hairpins, so I did what I could with a few braids and twists, my fingers remembering skills I'd thought they'd forgotten. When I was finished, I looked into the mirror.

The bodice of the dress was embroidered with roses, the thread only a few shades darker than the cloth so that I almost didn't notice them at first. The skirt was elegant and loose, not full like some of the styles I'd seen, and it did not drag on the floor. It was a dress made for a woman who did not need clothing to emphasize her beauty, and I realized with a jolt who this dress had been made for, who the clothes in the chest belonged to, whose room I had been sleeping in all of these months.

The ghost of the woman the Huntress had been stared at me out of the mirror, then faded, leaving only my own dazed expression. I sat on the bed with my earlier confidence shaken.

How would I feel if the Huntress showed up to dinner wearing my clothes?

There is a reason this dress feels unworn, I thought, stroking the skirt. *And there is a reason she brought me to this room, just as there is a reason the chest has contained almost everything I've needed so far.* The rose in my palm bloomed a darker shade of red, and I pressed it to my exposed chest, resting the rose over my heart. *And Aspen is right,* I thought, not bothering to glance back at the mirror. *Red is my color.*

I wrapped my wolf-skin cloak around my shoulders to keep off the chill and descended the steps down to the keep proper where I would find the Huntress, even if it meant looking beneath every drift in her forest. I would find her, and then . . . I did not know what I would do then.

Do you think she is the sort of woman to be overcome by tricks of light and cloth?

I was almost to the kitchen stairs when the wolf pup appeared, her jaws open in a wolfish laugh. She trotted off in the opposite direction toward the part of the keep that held the locked tower room. I followed, the rose in my hand pulsing with the strange magic of the place.

I found the Huntress in a large room that might have been a ballroom or an audience chamber or both. Part of the stone roof had fallen through, leaving a pile of moonlit rubble, and past the rubble, through a sparse fall of snow, was a throne. I froze when I saw her sprawled across it. She looked too natural there. It was like discovering that a dependable plow horse knew how to piaffe, except that the Huntress was as far from a plow horse as any living thing could be. She was royalty, or whatever the mountain equivalent of royalty might be. I had known that, in a way, for all that she had never told me who she'd been. She could read, and hunt, and she radiated power in a way I'd only seen in those born to it. Those traits led to only a few possible conclusions. Seeing her here, though, enthroned, was different. I *knew* the Huntress.

I did not know this woman.

I backed away, my soft shoes soundless on the floor, ashamed suddenly of my conviction. As a rich merchant's daughter, I had been good enough for a minor noble down on his luck or another wealthy merchant, but never someone like the woman

145

wearing the Huntress's face. The shame that had followed me ever since we'd fled the city washed over me in a hot, prickling wave.

"Rowan."

I kept walking.

"Rowan, wait."

Running footsteps echoed in the room, and it occurred to me through my desolate haze that this was the first time I had ever heard the Huntress's steps make a sound. I turned in surprise, and then she was close enough for me to see her eyes. They were rimmed with red and wild, and two high dots of color stained her cheekbones. I reached for her, unthinking.

"You," she said, as if she had only just realized who I was. "Rowan." Her eyes dropped to the dress, then back to my face. "Rowan," she said again, like it was the only word she knew.

"What is this room?" I asked her, still aware of the looming presence of the throne behind her. It seemed impossible that I had not discovered this place before, and at the thought the rose in my hand burned.

"My mother's throne room."

"Your mother."

"Yes. My mother. It doesn't matter now, though."

"Doesn't it?" I asked, my chin rising in defiance.

Her hair looked tangled, as if she had sat for hours with it balled up in her fists. "Why should it matter?"

"Because," I said, wishing I had never laid eyes on this dress, or this room, or the woman in front of me. "Because I keep thinking I know you, and then you go and do something like this."

"Like what?"

"Like remind me that you're something I can never have, no matter how much I want it, no matter how hard I try to tell myself I shouldn't even want it in the first place."

She looked at me like I'd driven a spear through her lungs. "Rowan."

"I should hate you, but I don't. I don't hate you, and I don't hate this place, and I want—"

146

The Huntress touched my face, and then her lips were on mine and my words fell to earth like spring snow, silent and inconsequential, as she kissed me. I wrapped my arms around her neck and pulled her closer. The throne faded, along with the rubble and the roses and my fears.

I opened my eyes when I felt light hit them. We stood beneath the crack in the ceiling, and above us, framed by scudding clouds, rose the moon.

"Wait." I pushed the Huntress away from me with every ounce of willpower I possessed.

She paused, her hand cupping the back of my neck, her face half lit by moonlight. "My name is Isolde," she said, answering the question I had not yet asked.

"Isolde." I tasted it and discarded it in the same instant. "You are not Isolde."

"No," she said. "Do you believe me now?"

"Yes." I moved to kiss her again, but she pulled away, a half-smile on the lips I wanted on my own.

"Dance with me."

"What?" I asked, tugging at the collar of her shirt.

"Dance with me. Now. Here." She stroked the embroidery along the sleeve of my dress.

"I was never a very good dancer," I said, remembering the parties I had gone to in the city, dancing with too many men with too many hands while my eyes followed the women around us.

"It doesn't matter." She moved, her step as light and careful as it was in the woods, dancing with death with a spear in her hand. I moved with her, one hand on her shoulder, one hand on her waist. Had I been in the city, I would have placed my hands differently, but when I tried to adjust she shook her head.

"Just like this." Her position mirrored mine, and I followed her steps while the wind whistled over the crack in the roof, making its own music. "You surprised me," she said. "For a moment, I did not recognize you."

"I should not have worn the dress."

She pulled me to her with a complicated series of steps that caught me off guard. I felt her heart beating against mine as she spoke.

"I would know you in anything, Rowan. And I am very glad you wore it." She grinned at me, and my heart skipped a beat as the woman I knew returned. "It was a trick of the moonlight and old ghosts. This side of the keep is full of them."

I let her spin me away and bring me back, my feet finding the steps while the room blurred around me, the Huntress the only fixed point.

"Then why do you come here?" I asked, breathless.

"To remind myself."

"But you're not Isolde anymore."

"Maybe not," she said, wrapping her arms around me slowly, her steps sure and easy as she lifted me into the air. Snow brushed my throat, and I tasted moonlight like pale wine. "But I'm here because of her, and so are you."

She lowered me, and I clung to her neck, still drunk. "Why did you run from me?" I said, my lips brushing her skin with each word.

She ran her hands down my side, and I moved against her, desire rising to meet her touch. "Run?"

"You changed earlier. And you've run from me before."

"So have you," she said. "But it doesn't matter. I can't run from you now."

"And why is that?" I struggled to focus on her words instead of her hands.

"Do you really have to ask?"

"It's the dress, isn't it," I said, only half-teasing. There was power at work here. I could feel it in the beat of my heart, blood rushing through veins ringed with briars, and in the walls of this room with its tattered tapestries and old banners. The Huntress kissed me, and the wind picked up, whipping snow down through the moonlight.

"It's not the dress." She laced her fingers through mine and led me into another dance.

I was out of breath and flushed by the time our steps led us to the door.

"Wine?" she asked.

I didn't want wine. I wanted the lips that had formed the word, but I nodded.

She did not offer me her arm, as Avery or one of my father's acquaintances might have. I was glad of it. Instead, she took my hand with the same grace she did everything, making it look as natural as breathing. Maybe it was. I tightened my fingers around hers and did not look back.

"Wait here," she said outside the kitchen door. "I'll get the wine."

But where will we drink it? I wondered as I waited in the dark of the hallway, thinking of the room above the stable and a bed piled high with furs.

The library, as it turned out.

The Huntress lit the fire in the grate, then laid a fur before it. I shivered. "Sit," she said, as the silver and black hairs of the pelt rippled in the flames. She shrugged out of her leathers, leaving only the fine wool of her shirt between me and her skin as she settled onto the floor. I watched the cloth rise and fall with her breathing, the firelight warm on the exposed skin of my chest.

"Are you human?" I asked her.

"Would it matter?"

I met her eyes, and this time I didn't see forests. I just saw her. "No," I said, my voice rough. I didn't care what she was or who she had been; I just wanted her.

She leaned back to look at me, and I did not blush under her gaze as it traveled down my throat.

"I don't want you to leave," she said, and I felt the swell of mountains in her voice. "I want you to stay here with me."

I slid the sleeve of my dress over one shoulder, my heart racing as I spoke. "Always."

She closed her eyes, her lips parted over words she did not say aloud, and suddenly I did not want her tenderness or the gentle heat of the flames. I wanted the Huntress, and the Huntress was

149

ice and snow and shattered light. I pulled her to me, startling her eyes open, and kissed her hard as the weight of her body settled over me.

She answered, her lips moving down my neck to my shoulder, then farther down, and I wrapped my legs around her as she tugged the gown lower. The wool was sturdy and did not tear, and she let out a growl of frustration that sounded so much like a wolf I would have laughed if it had not unleashed a new wave of desire. She raised me up, her fingers as deft on the laces as they were on a bowstring, and I let her lift the dress over my head before lying back on the softness of the furs to let her look at me. I could feel her eyes, and at last I felt her hands, gentle again as she ran them down my sides and over the arch of ribs and hips until I ached for her to touch me with each shuddering breath.

"Please," I said, and I remembered, as she slid inside me, that please was one of the first words I'd ever said to her, and then the world opened around me as she moved with my body and I remembered nothing else for a long, long while.

Days turned into weeks turned into months.

She had not kept track of time when the witch first brought her world to ruin, and there had been no point afterward. There were no seasons to mark the year, only winter, endless and unchanging and as familiar as loss. Time was inconsequential. She had so much of it.

But years had passed, for all that she did not know how many. The keep provided her with what little she needed, the cellars never quite running dry, the garden never quite giving up, and the scent of baking bread never quite abandoning the ovens. There had been a time when she hated the witch for those small mercies. Each was a reminder that the body she wore was human, and each tied her, albeit loosely, to a life she longed to forget. In time, the hatred too had passed, turning into a bitter gratitude that she tried not to think about, just as she ignored the passing of the years while she herself remained unchanged.

Now, though, the days lined up behind her like a silent army, grim and determined, secure in the knowledge that their numbers gave them the advantage.

Rowan was mortal.

The years would steal her, little by little, and the happiness she'd found would blow like snow away over the mountains. The rose had rooted, and blossomed. So the witch had promised.

These thoughts only came to her in moments like these, when the north wind howled and clawed against the shutters, calling for her and raging when she did not answer. She could not, not with Rowan sleeping in her arms, not with death so close already. She could only wait for the night to pass and dawn to bring Rowan back to her, free of ghosts and curses, the light promising only the sweet, sharp taste of joy.

151

Chapter Sixteen

A twig snapped somewhere in the frozen forest. I knew the difference now between the crack of frozen sap and the careful tread of game. The wolf crouched beside me. Her ears swiveled, listening to something out of the range of my own hearing, and I watched her watch the woods, relying on her stronger senses.

She no longer bore any resemblance to the scrawny sack of fur and bones I had scooped up off the stable floor. Her shoulders came to my hip, still smaller than her siblings, but larger than any dog I had ever seen. White frosted the black fur around her ruff, and her muzzle was darker than shadow, a sharp contrast to the gleam of teeth beneath.

I checked the string of my bow. We had been tracking a herd of deer for the better part of a day, and the Huntress was somewhere over the next rise with the rest of the pack. I had circled back to startle them into flight, driving them down the slope and into the jaws of the waiting wolves. I stepped carefully, avoiding a deep drift, my muscles hard beneath my furs and my breath coming easily even in the frigid air. I heard only the crunch of snow beneath my boots. I followed the low plume of the wolf's tail as she trotted through the trees after a scent far too faint for my nose to detect. I knew some of the smells of these woods. There was the sweet musk of deer, and the heavier scent of elk. The raw eye-watering stench of bear, and the harsh odor of wildcat urine. At the edges of these scents hovered the clean, clear smell of snow, and the peculiar difference between snow, running water, and ice.

And roses.

I hesitated, raising my face to the wind. The boundary was close; I had not realized we had come so far, but then again, the boundary did not seem to obey the laws of nature as I understood them.

The wolf's hackles rose. I breathed the air in through my nose, trying to catch wind of the source of her alarm. The smell of roses was heavier here, and sure enough as we padded over a ridge, I saw the hedge rise into view.

We both froze.

There were no deer, over the ridge, but something moved. It took my eyes a long time to remember the shape. The creature looked so awkward, shuffling through the snow with its mottled pelt and its strange burden. Each step was clearly a labor, and it eyed the hedge with grim determination. Something stirred in the back of my mind, crawling out from the place where I had shoved such things, buried under the weight of snow and fur and the Huntress's body, burned away by cold and moonlight and the warm red glow of the hearth, and drowned by the sound and fury of the storms that shrieked over the peaks.

The old woman crouched over her pack, unloading it into the shelter of the briars. She was careful, excruciatingly careful, her every move slow and steady as she kept her body clear of thorns.

I crept down the hill, keeping to the shadows of the trees and trusting the snow to hide the sound of my passage. The wolf kept pace. I wondered if she could smell my fear, or if the stench was trapped beneath my furs. This was the first other human being I had seen since I was taken. I tried to remember how long ago that would have been. The effort hurt. I remembered the pup, but not when she had grown. I remembered her first kill: a rabbit, white of fur and dark of eye, but not when she had made it. I remembered the Huntress's hands, guiding my own along the bowstring, but I did not remember when the bow had become an extension of my arm, or when reaching for an arrow had become easier than reaching for a word. The rose in my bloodstream stirred. I was used to that now too.

I should speak to her.

The thought made me tremble, and I could not stop the shaking. I put my hand on the wolf's shoulder for support and stepped out from behind a tree.

She saw me. The hedge rose between us, but it was thin here and seemed to part before me the longer I stared at it.

"Lady," the woman said, sinking to her knees and bowing her head.

I did not know what to say. I stared at her bowed head, wrapped in a thick, woolen scarf, and felt the icy walls I'd built up around my memories of home begin to thaw. Terror gripped my stomach. I needed those walls.

"What are you doing here?" I asked. The words felt thick on my tongue.

The woman looked up. She was older than my father, her skin the brown of ripe acorns and wrinkled from too many years in the sun and cold. "Remembering," she said. Her eyes were Lockland blue.

"Remembering what?"

"Many things, child. Many winters." She gestured to the ground before her, and I looked at what she had brought. Small bundles of sticks, almost doll-like, bound with scraps of cloth or bits of hair, lay in the snow. I recoiled.

"What are they?"

"The memories of others. I bring them here on midwinter."

"Why?"

"Because that is my job, child. I carry the memories of the dead so that the people in my care may set them aside."

"You are a hedgewitch."

"Of course. This boy here," she said, lifting a small figurine wrapped in a bit of green ribbon, "died of fever a fortnight past. The winter dead belong to the mountain."

I remembered the story the Huntress had told me about the significance of the winter rose to mothers.

"Why did you call me lady?"

"You belong to the mountain. It pays to be respectful." She gave me a shrewd look and pulled out another wooden bundle. A strip of yellow silk clothed its chest, and something about the color made my throat go dry.

"Who is that one for?" I asked.

"This is for a man whose body has outlived his soul, his daughters say. He was a merchant once, proud and powerful. Now he sinks deeper and deeper into madness, speaking only of roses. His daughters begged me for help, and I will tell you what I told them. This man will never forgive himself. His heart already belongs to the mountain, and he will die before the spring unless he can find a reason to live."

"A merchant?" The world went gray, then yellow as the silk.

"Yes. A merchant with three daughters, though only two remain to him. I have brought this here in the hopes that some small mercy might be granted him."

Father.

"What of his daughters?"

"One is married, the other still too young to wed."

"Who did she marry then?"

The hedgewitch placed the figure on the snow and gave me a smile with too many teeth. "You know his name, child." She turned to go.

"Wait," I screamed after her, but she did not, and her hunched form faded into the forest while the roses whispered and the life I'd chosen shattered like glass.

My father was dying. Madness, the witch had said, but I did not think it was madness. Guilt, perhaps, and grief, one too many losses piled up on his broad shoulders. He had been quietly breaking since my mother's death, diminishing, fading, desperation turning him into a stranger. Now he feared his eldest daughter dead or worse, and he had given up at last while Aspen married Avery to keep the family fed and Juniper. . .

I had to return.

I had bought myself time, here in the wilds, but I had been a fool to think I could escape forever. My family needed me, and perhaps my presence would give my father the strength he needed to survive the winter.

And if not?

I gazed at the roses, seeing another casket, another time. If I could not save him, then I had to see him. I had to say goodbye. I had to tell him I forgave him, even if he couldn't forgive himself.

Then I would return to the Huntress.

The wolf turned her head to look me in the eyes, and there was a message there that I could not read and was not sure I wanted to.

Something shifted. The wolves were restless, and there was a strange edge to the air.

Rowan should be back by now.

A strange coppery taste filled her mouth, and she recognized it for what it was: fear. The girl could have met anything in the forest, stumbled upon a bear, or a lynx, or . . . The scent of roses flooded her nostrils, drowning out all else.

No.

The Huntress dropped her spear and ran, racing toward the boundary and the end of everything.

She found Rowan on her knees, staring into the thorns.

"I have to go," she said, and the Huntress listened to the story that spilled from the girl's lips, a torrent of words rushing like meltwater.

The Huntress closed her eyes. In the darkness behind her lids, she heard the sound she had been dreading since she followed an old man down the mountain to a tiny cottage on the edge of Locke's old land. It was barely audible, more of a hush than a noise, a whisper of a whisper, the sound the wind makes before it starts to blow. It was the sound of a single petal falling.

She saw a body on the spring grass, roses red as blood across a broken chest.

"The price of freedom will be the loss of one you cannot bear to lose."

The pieces fell into place.

"Go," she told Rowan, gathering the girl into her arms. "Go to your father."

She could not have designed a better trap if she had been given a century to think on it. If she refused to let Rowan go, the girl would

157

grow to hate her over time, and the ending would be the same. She
would lose her, just as surely as she was about to lose her now.

"I will come back," said Rowan, tears in her eyes. "I will come back
to you. I swear it."

The Huntress kissed her. She tasted like spring and rain and roses,
not the cold white roses that surrounded them, but the heady smell of
wild roses blooming along hedgerows, heavy with summer, and the
ponderous, many-petaled heads of the roses grown in the gardens of
the wealthy, overflowing with abundance.

"I will be here," she said, forcing herself to let Rowan go, forcing
herself to smile. She removed the bundle of food she'd packed for the
hunt from her belt and pressed it into Rowan's hands. "This should
last you. It is only a three-day journey on foot. Follow the slope of the
hills, and bring the wolf. She'll keep you safe."

"Thank you," Rowan said, kissing her one last time.

The Huntress turned away. She couldn't stop Rowan, but she did
not have to see the hope flare to life in the girl's dark eyes. She did not
have to see the reflection of her breaking heart.

A rose for a rose, a thorn for a thorn.

Rowan might return, but the Huntress would be gone, the curse at
last unraveled.

Chapter Seventeen

Snow fell. I welcomed it, because snow dimmed the light of the world and muffled the sharp edges, sounds fading, even the feel of the earth lost beneath countless feet of snow. The wolf led; I followed. That first night, heat from the fire melted the snow on the overhanging branches of a nearby pine, and then it froze again, dangling from the boughs in long teeth of ice. They brushed against me every time I stood to fetch more wood.

Winter still has her teeth.

The fire did not warm me. I stared into it instead and remembered.

My mother died one morning in early autumn when the leaves in her garden had just begun to turn and the rosehips were still firm and tart and not yet ripe for picking. The wasting illness had stripped her bare, until the woman in the bed was nothing more than a whiff of perfume, a memory of passage, the essence of a life distilled into paper-thin skin and too-large eyes. The only thing the sickness left her was her voice.

"Take care of them, Rowan. You must be strong, and you must believe that I am with you always. There will be days where you will want nothing more than to run from the weight of your strength, but you must learn to bear it because that is what it means to grow up. I had hoped to spare you that a little longer."

She had squeezed my hand, and the fierceness of her grip surprised me.

159

"Mothers are not supposed to have favorites, but you will always be my firstborn daughter, and there was a time when I loved you more than anything else in the world. You must love your sisters now for me and forgive your father, for he is a good man, but he does not have your strength."

I had tried. I had given them all I could, but I had run from it in the end, just like my mother had warned me I would.

A stick fell, sparking, and I shielded my eyes against the light. *She would have understood,* I thought. She too had fled from a life she hadn't wanted. She had left the village of her birth to live in a city by the sea, carrying only the cutting of the mountain rose she'd planted in a stranger's garden. That she had come to love that stranger did not make her choice any easier, or the risk any less great.

Now my father was dying, and the only thing that would save him from himself was my forgiveness.

The wind roared through the trees. I listened for the howl of wolves, but only the branches of the pines replied. I bit down hard on my cheek and on my disappointment. For all the pain it would have caused me, I had not wanted the Huntress to let me go.

It did not get easier. The second day brought more snow, and the wind pushed against me, roaring up the mountain towards the keep and threatening to take me with it. The wolf's ears lay flat against her skull, her eyes yellow slits between her lids. Each step cost me something, but by the end of the day neither the Huntress nor what awaited me in the village was at the forefront of my mind.

It was cold. There was no way I could light a fire in a storm like this, and so I burrowed under the sheltering branches of a pine, scooping out a hollow for me and the wolf. I forced myself to crawl back out once more, knife in hand, to cut pine boughs to lay upon the snow. They would at least prevent the ground from leaching the heat out of my body.

The smell of the needles sent a stab of longing through me as I lay with the wolf pressed against my back.

The storm continued into the third day, and again we stumbled down the mountain, the words of the Huntress echoing in my head. My three-day journey was nowhere near its conclusion. I could not see where I was going, and so I trusted to the wolf, hoping she had the sense to avoid triggering an avalanche or walking us off a cliff.

We found game by accident. I stepped on the rabbit, and its back broke beneath my boot. It must have been scurrying along some hidden tunnel, thinking itself safe beneath the snow, just like I had been before the old woman found me. I finished the job, then fed it to the wolf. I would have to make do with the dried meat in my pack, since there was no guarantee tonight would yield a fire on which to cook the rabbit and I was not hungry enough to eat raw meat quite yet.

I regretted the decision a few hours later. The snow slowed enough for a small blaze, and by dawn the sky had cleared and I roasted a few vegetables in the coals, softening a strip of dried meat in my mouth while I waited. I tried not to think about the meal I would have eaten back at the keep. In the howling darkness, free from the spell of the Huntress's presence, I wondered if the food there was enchanted like the stories old women told about the forest fae who tempted lost children with feasts that lasted a thousand years and made the children forget where they had come from while their mothers wept over empty cribs. It was always the mothers who suffered most in those stories. The children seemed happy enough.

If only I had stayed away from the boundary, I thought, the dull ache in my chest spreading. *If only I had stayed asleep.*

On the fourth day, I came across the road. Ruts from logging teams turned my ankles beneath the snow, but I welcomed the pain. Where there were roads, there were people.

The clank of trace chains warned me of their presence long before they saw me. A woodsman and a young boy whom I took to be his son walked behind an old dray horse hitched to a log. The horse caught the wolf's scent and shifted nervously, tossing its head. The wolf, for her part, took on a stalking stiff-legged curiosity that should have served as a warning to me, but did not.

"Which way is Three Elms?" I asked, stepping out from the trees with my hand on the wolf's hackles.

The man shoved the boy behind him, fumbling for the crossbow dangling from the harness hames.

"Wait!" I put myself between him and the wolf, cursing my own stupidity. "I'm lost. I mean you no harm. Three Elms?"

He pointed down the road, his hands still gripping the weapon, and as I nodded my thanks I saw him make the sign against the evil eye. My shoulder blades prickled for a long time, waiting for his bolt to land. "I should not have brought you," I told the wolf.

We stayed in the woods after that. It felt safer, and for all that the road was familiar it was also strange to see it cutting through the trees after so many weeks of unbroken forest. The woods were free of people, at least, and the snow lay heavy on the ground. Something about that bothered me, but I couldn't place it, and I was too hungry to care too much. Game animals made themselves scarce this close to the villages and I was out of food.

We were on the trail of a pheasant when the woods opened before me, catching me off guard. I stopped at the edge of the clearing, my eyes wide as they took in the sweep of yard and the dark wood of the barn. Past the barn, past the well with its mound of snow, stood the cottage. It looked just as it had when I had left it, only without smoke in the chimney. No light escaped through the cracks in the shutters, and nothing stirred in the barn. The wolf sniffed the air once, then trotted over the snow, leaving large canine prints behind her. These too unsettled me, until I realized that I was standing where the wolf had stood the day I looked up from the well and saw the yellow eyes and white fur of Winter's hounds.

"And now I'm back," I told the silent clearing. The words felt even hollower than they sounded.

The door opened at my touch. I knew the house was empty,

but that did nothing to lessen the sharp ache of disappointment. No cloaks hung from the rack by the door, and no boots slouched against the wall. I ran my hands along the door itself, my fingers finding the places where the door had splintered beneath the bear's assault. Someone had repaired it, but that someone no longer lived here.

Inside, the house was tidy, unlike the Huntress's keep, but for all that leaves and bones gathered in the corners of those halls, this house still felt emptier. The kitchen table had a fine layer of dust on it, and the vase where the rose had bloomed in frost was nowhere to be seen. The wolf sniffed at the floor, pausing by the hearth where my father's chair watched, the battered leather oddly sentient.

I wandered into the bedroom I had shared with my sisters. The pallets had been stripped of sheets, and no clothes remained in the chest. Not even mine. I wondered at this, then decided it didn't matter. I knew where my family was. Their clothes were no doubt with them.

The rose twisted, and I gasped in pain as a thousand thorns pierced me. It was over by the time I drew my next breath, but I held my hand up to the dim light of dusk, staring at the smooth skin.

She let you go. You knew there would be a price to pay.

I would pay it later. First, I had to find my father.

I walked through the house one more time, running my hands over the familiar surfaces and trying not to feel like I was memorizing every detail. It was the kind of house a person could love, once that person moved past memories of richly decorated town houses, dead mothers, lost friends, and freedom. The walls were sturdy and the roof was sound, and someone had carved roses around the door frame. I paused, running my finger along the trim. I didn't remember that detail from before, but the work was old and polished with oil from generations of hands. It reminded me of my mother's garden.

Part of bookkeeping, my father had explained to me as a child, was seeing patterns. It was not enough to add neat columns of figures. A good bookkeeper could see stories in the numbers, just like a poem. A dishonest bookkeeper could tell stories with those numbers, making them lie, but there was an art to that, too. I wondered, my hands tracing a petal, if the answers I had sought about the Huntress had been waiting here the entire time. My mother's roses had been nothing like the roses that grew around the Huntress's keep. They were lush and warm and inclined to brown and die in winter, instead of breeding ice, but my mother was an ordinary woman. No magic ran in her veins, and yet . . .

"Why do roses symbolize love?" I had asked my mother one morning as I watched her pruning back the canes. She sat on her heels, pulling off one of the thick leather gloves she wore to protect herself, and showed me a scar.

"Love is beautiful, like the rose," she said, still staring at her hand. "It blossoms with care, but requires tending. There are many different types of roses, just as there are types of love. Some large, some small, some fragrant, some merely decorative. There are roses that bloom by the sea in poor soil, and those that need rich soils and gentle climates. But the real reason that roses symbolize love is right here." She had brushed a thorn with her bare finger, letting it dimple her skin.

"Thorns?"

"Indeed. You are too young for romantic love, but think about Aspen."

"I hate Aspen." Aspen had, earlier that day, pinched me hard enough to leave a bruise.

"You love your sister; you don't hate her. But she is hard to love sometimes, isn't she? Love is like that. Beautiful, intoxicating even, but sharp as broken glass. You must handle it as you would a rose. Gently, knowing when to prune and when to water, and you must never grasp a cane too tightly, or it will cut you."

"That sounds terrible."

"Love can be terrible."

"But you love father. Is he terrible?"

"Your father is a wonderful man, Rowan. But you can love

someone wonderful so much it hurts, just like I love you. And you can love someone terrible." She had pulled me close and kissed the top of my head, and I had lost interest in the subject.

The words came back to me now with a wave of fierce grief. My mother's garden, the thorn in my palm, the Huntress's briars, her story about the winter rose—they were all connected somehow, only I wasn't clever enough to see it.

Cold.

She raised her hand to the falling snow, letting the flakes pile up on her bare skin. It had been years since she had been cold. The sensation startled her, novel in its discomfort, a welcome distraction from the emptiness that filled each waking moment and stalked her dreams.

She had been content here, once.

Now she saw Rowan each time she closed her eyes. At night she lay beside her ghost, and the ache inside her grew until she gave up on sleep and watched the clouds chase the moon.

The cold crept in further.

Death was mercy in the mountains, and cold the gentlest way to die. Was this what the witch had meant by freedom? She would die here, alone at the top of the world, and the curse would end with her life.

All this, for nothing.

No.

Not nothing.

The Huntress closed her fist around the snow, remembering a laugh, a touch, the taste of happiness. Not even a lifetime would have been enough.

The snow melted, running down her wrist, and with it immortality.

Chapter Eighteen

The setting sun cast my shadow before me as I followed the dirt track into the village and up to the Locklands' door. I heard the whispers following me, and the sound of shutters and doors opening as I put one foot in front of the other, meeting my shadow with every step. The wolf stayed close. I had wanted to lock her in the cottage, but my hand had hesitated on the latch and she had bolted out, baring her teeth.

Let them see, I decided. I was thankful for that decision, now that the entire village had turned out to stare. If I had felt out of place here before the Huntress had taken me, it was nothing to how I felt today.

The Lockland lodge was a huge, sprawling house that had been added on to over the years as the family grew. At one point, I guessed, there had been real wealth here, but that day was long gone. What was left was carefully maintained, but rough, just like the rest of the village. I raised the stag's head knocker on the broad doors and let it fall, once, twice, three times. The sound echoed in the stillness of twilight.

A young woman opened it a few heartbeats later, her cheeks flushed and her lips still wearing a lingering laugh that died when she saw the wolf. The smells of sweat and ale washed over me, and I felt my own hackles rise in response.

"I need to talk to Aspen," I said, not bothering with courtesies. The girl's face paled, and she glanced over her shoulder.

"Who is it?" A male voice asked. The woman wet her lips, fear radiating from her pores, and didn't answer.

"Aspen," I said to her again, keeping my voice low. "Now."

I had not thought about the consequences of my return. My father was dying; that was enough to compel me, but the fear in her face awoke an answering fear in my own heart. I had been gone for months. Long enough for spring to come and go and winter to come again. Long enough for Aspen to marry, and long enough for my family to mourn me as dead. Long enough for suspicion to take root where joy might once have bloomed.

"Just someone here to see Aspen." She took a step away from me, her eyes glued to the wolf.

"It's colder than the Huntress's tits out there, girl. Shut the goddamn door." Heavy footsteps approached, and then I was looking up into the blue eyes and bushy beard of one of Avery's cousins. His glare turned to terror as the wolf growled, and I worried for a moment that he might piss himself. "Avery," he called over his shoulder. "Someone get Avery."

The girl slipped away, and I willed her to find my sister before this man thought to put a crossbow bolt through my heart. Behind me I could hear the gathering crowd.

"Rowan!"

I turned, my heart catching in my throat. A girl stood no more than ten feet away from me with her arms full of groceries. She was even taller than I remembered, and she wore her dark hair pulled over one shoulder in a long braid threaded through with ribbons. I took a half step toward her, then another, unsure. "Juniper?"

"It *is* you."

My youngest sister looked at me out of a face that had lost the fat of childhood. Her eyes brimmed with tears, and she was in the process of putting down her basket when another familiar voice poured cold dread down my spine.

"Rowan."

I turned to face my former fiancé, words dying in my throat.

He, too, was taller than I remembered, and he had grown a black beard like his cousin's. It suited him.

"Avery," I said, trying to keep my voice steady. As always, the dread I felt before seeing him had me trembling with doubt at the sight of his face. Beauty was so deceptive. He smiled his easy smile, looking every inch the headman's son.

"We thought you were dead. Or ran off to your city. Some of us thought you'd run off to your city *and* died. But," he said, looking me up and down, "here you are. Alive."

"Where is my sister?"

"My wife is inside."

"And my father?"

"I'm afraid your father is not well."

"Bring me to them." I dug my hands into the wolf's fur as Avery's eyes flashed at my presumption.

"Where have you been, Rowan?" he asked.

"I want to see my father." I was all too aware of the rising murmur of the watching crowd.

"We thought you were dead," he said again. There was an odd emotion there. Anger, maybe, or regret.

"I'm not."

"Tell me where you have been then, and I will let you see your father."

"Don't you know?" I asked, looking from him to Juniper. "Didn't my father tell you?"

The emotions wrestling on his face coalesced into something more familiar: disbelief. "The Huntress is a fairy tale."

I had nothing to say to this. It had never occurred to me, not once in the time since I had been taken, that the villagers might not believe the story told by my family. "Your father came down from the mountain sick with madness. It happens."

"Your father crossed the boundary, Avery," I said, speaking the first words that came into my head. The crowd gave a collective hiss.

"No." Avery's face darkened. "My father respected the old ways."

"Who do you think the boundary protects?" I nearly shouted. "Why do you think there is a boundary at all, or old ways, if not for the Huntress?"

"Say you're right then," he said, his voice tight. "Say the Huntress killed my father and my brother, as your father claims. Why did she release you?"

"Because—" I broke off, mind racing. *Because she loves me,* but that was not something I could say to the man who I was once to wed.

"How do I know you're who you say you are, and not some trick?"

"Trick? Avery." His name burst from my lips, and he flinched as if I'd struck him. "You can't explain me away, Avery."

The sounds of the crowd faded, and for a moment it was just the two of us. I remembered, with a twinge of regret, the small things Avery had done for me over the months I had known him. The carved wolf, the walks around the village where his pride in his home had soured to bitterness each time I looked down on what I saw with scorn.

"I've never been able to explain you," he said, but I did not have time for what might have been.

"Rowan?" Aspen appeared at Avery's elbow, her dark eyes wide. He placed a protective arm around her shoulders, and I couldn't help staring at the swell of her stomach. Aspen. Pregnant. It didn't seem possible, and I reeled as I understood what my mind had tried to tell me. I really had been gone a year, from one midwinter to another.

"You're alive," she said. Then she saw the wolf. Something flashed across her face too quickly for me to read, but I saw her place a hand on Avery's arm with a deliberation that held meaning, even if I could not tell what that meaning was.

"How is father?" I asked her.

The expression that I could not read flashed again, and she frowned. "Dying. You're too late, Rowan."

The chill in her voice forced me back a step, and the wolf looked up at me with questioning eyes. "I—"

171

"You should go back to wherever you came from," Aspen said. "There is no place for you here."

"Aspen—"

"Go, Rowan. Juniper, get inside before that creature rips out your throat."

Juniper obeyed, looking just as confused as I felt. Even Avery seemed taken aback, but he allowed his wife to pull him back into the warmth of the lodge. Aspen shut the door on me herself, and I heard the thud of a bar falling across it. I stared at the dark wood, stunned and aching and more tired than I'd ever felt in my life.

The crowd parted before me, and I did not dare to meet their eyes. They were not throwing stones yet, but I did not trust these people. The wolf pointed her nose toward the forest, and I hesitated, the temptation to vanish into the trees strong. I watched her lope into the woods, the wind rippling the fur along her back, while I followed the road back to the cottage.

I collapsed in front of the cold hearth. My eyes saw nothing and I heard only the rustle of thorn against thorn until a soft knock on the door roused me from a lapse in consciousness that bore little resemblance to sleep. I held my breath, listening, and then Juniper's voice called my name.

"Can I come in?" Juniper's lower lip quivered with suppressed emotion when I opened the door.

I stepped back, afraid to speak, afraid to break the spell of her presence.

"It's freezing in here," Juniper said. "Let me light the fire." She checked that all the shutters were tightly latched, then laid a small fire in the hearth with shaking hands. "I brought you some bread and cheese and sausage."

"Aspen," I began, but Juniper cut me off.

"Ignore her. She didn't mean it. Not really. I think she was trying to protect you."

"Protect me? By telling me to leave?"

"You don't know what it's been like since you left."

The accusation hurt.

"Since I left? Do you think I wanted to leave?"

"No! Of course not. Rowan, eat something, please. You look half starved. I brought something for your . . . your friend, too." She pulled out another bundle, and I smelled the clean, coppery scent of blood as she unwrapped a meaty bone.

"Juniper." I wanted to hug her, but something held me back. It was too strange, being back in this house without Aspen or my father. "What happened?"

"After . . . after you left, Father went mad. That's why no one believes him. He wouldn't stop talking about roses and bears and a woman with a bone-white spear. Aspen tried to tell Avery the truth, but he didn't want to listen. Aspen says he's afraid of the truth. It was . . . it was easier after a while to forget what we saw and just go along with him."

"What does he believe then?"

"He believes his father and brother were killed in an avalanche, and that Father was hit in the head. He believes you ran away to the city afterward because without Father nobody could force you to marry him."

I might have done, I thought. "They crossed the boundary and killed the Huntress's Hounds."

Juniper looked at me like I, too, was crazy. "I don't know what the Hounds are," she said, her eyes beseeching me, "but Avery says that no one here would ever cross the boundary, which is why it could not have been the Huntress."

"He called her a fairy tale. How can he not believe in her but believe in the boundary?"

Juniper took a deep breath. "Because if his father crossed the boundary, then that means it was his father's fault he and Avery's brother died, and his fault that you were taken, and Avery can't accept that."

"But you remember," I said, reaching for her hand. "You remember the truth."

"Of course I do." She trembled. "I will remember it as long as I live. How did you get away?"

"She let me go."

173

"Why?"

"I met an old woman in the woods. A hedgewitch, I think. She told me father was sick, and so the Huntress let me come back."

Juniper gave me a wary look.

"She just let you go?"

"She's not a monster, Juniper."

"She killed people and stole you away from us because father picked a flower."

"She—" How could I explain what the Huntress was, or why she had done what she had done, to someone who did not know her?

"Avery says that if the Huntress really did take you, then you must be bewitched."

"I'm not," I said, thinking of the rose in my palm.

"He said you wouldn't know it, if you were. Don't you see? Why else would you return, almost a year from the day you were taken?"

"Because the old woman told me father was dying. Do you think I'm bewitched?"

"I don't know. I am so happy to see you, Rowan, but it feels too good to be true. Just like the dreams I had right after mother died, and then I'd wake up, and she'd still be dead. What am I supposed to think?"

"That I'm your sister," I said, grasping her shoulders in my hands and looking her in the eyes. "And that I'm back."

She blinked up at me through tears. "Okay," she said. "I believe you. But what are you going to tell Avery?"

I took strength from her presence and gritted my teeth.

"The truth."

The wolves howled outside the keep, calling to her.

She did not answer.

The window in the tallest tower commanded a view over her entire world, from forest to lake to sheltered glen. Somewhere down there was Rowan.

Rage built.

The tower room had served another purpose, once. She did not remember what it had been, only that it was irrelevant, now, but this high up it still preserved the voices of the dead, echoing in the soft stir of flower and vine.

Queen among the bones.

She would have ruled these mountains with the same cold fury she felt now, stretching her territory to the foothills and beyond, raiding all the way to the coast. That had been her destiny, another thing the witch had stolen and replaced with ice. She reached for a storm, willing the clouds to roil into snow, but the sky refused to answer.

The breaking of her power rolled over her like the storm that had not come. Below, the wolves howled on, speaking in a language that felt as foreign to her now as the tongue they spoke across the sea. She slid to the ground. She did not remember the stones being this cold, or the cost of each breath so high.

I am dying, she realized, lifting her face toward the light. I am dying, and I cannot outrun this fate or fight it off. I am the hunted now.

Chapter Nineteen

"Avery Lockland." My words reverberated in the darkness as I pounded on the Lockland door. A storm was coming. I felt it in the sharp cold of the air and the silence in the trees. The scent of roses flooded my nostrils, and I could hardly hear the footsteps coming to the door for the rustling of those hidden leaves.

Avery answered. He was still dressed for the day's work, his dark shirtsleeves rolled up over corded forearms. "What do you want, Rowan?" he said.

"I want to see my father."

"You should have thought about that before you ran away from us."

"I did not run from you," I said.

He let out a bitter laugh that reminded me of the Huntress. "I would have been good to you, you know," he said.

It was not what I had expected him to say. I thought about Juniper's words, and wondered how far Avery would go for the sake of injured pride. "You would have tried, Avery, and you would have grown to hate me. You do see that, don't you? Aspen was always the better choice."

At my words, she appeared behind him, her hands on her pregnant belly and her eyes wide with fear.

For me, or for Avery?

"Yes," he said, some of the darkness lifting from his face as he looked at my sister. "But we were never given much of a choice, were we?"

"No."

"I will let you see your father. But you have to tell me the truth."

"The truth," I repeated. That was, after all, what I had come here to do.

"About where you've been all these months, and about what happened to my father and brother."

"You know where I've been. My father told you. My sisters told you. Tell him, Aspen."

Aspen remained mute, her knuckles white on her stomach. *Her fear is not for me or for Avery,* I suddenly understood. *She is afraid for her child.*

"Fine," I said, pulling off my mitten and stepping further into the light. I held up my palm for Avery to see and watched the color drain from his face as he saw the rose bloom beneath my skin.

"This is the truth, Avery Lockland. Your father and your brother crossed the boundary. They did not tell my father what it meant, and so he plucked a single rose for his oldest daughter while your family killed two of the Huntress's wolves. She killed them for it, and she spared my father, not knowing about the rose he had hidden in his cloak until he had returned. She came for the rose then, and she took me, too. Do not blame my father for the mistakes of yours."

Rage twisted his handsome features. "It was your father who led mine into the mountains. Your father who poisoned him with empty promises."

"Yes," I said, lowering my hand. "But my father did not know what else roamed the snows."

"Or perhaps he didn't listen."

I flinched, considering this possibility, then caught Aspen's eye. *Please,* her face seemed to say.

"Avery," I said, trying to soften my voice and reminding myself that in the end he had lost more than I. "I am sorry for what happened to your family, but my father did not lie to you. Please, let me see him."

"She speaks the truth."

All four of us started, turning to peer into the darkness. A woman stepped into the light, her weathered face familiar beneath its hood.

"You," I said, recognizing the woman from the boundary.

"You know the old stories, Avery Lockland. She is marked by thorns."

Avery looked horrified, for a moment, and then something in his face changed. "Her hand," he said, pointing at me.

"Show me, child." I turned over my naked palm, a warning prickling the hairs along the back of my neck. "There is only one reason why the Huntress would let this woman go, Avery Lockland, and you know it as well as I."

Avery looked from me to the old woman. Comprehension dawned on his face slowly. "You may see your father." He moved aside. "Aspen will take you."

"Wait," I said, the feeling of apprehension growing stronger. "Avery."

My sister reached for my hand and pulled me into the house. "This way," she said. "Father doesn't have much time."

The lodge was nearly empty at this hour, and she led me to a small room at the back. The air was heavy with the smells of smoke and herbs, and Aspen lit a candle to illuminate the sickroom and the man sleeping on the narrow bed against the wall. My stomach turned. This was not my father. This was an old man, with hair the gray of dirty snow and his back bent beneath the weight of tragedy. His skin, even in the warm glow of the candle, looked ashen, and his eyes, when they opened, were cloudy.

"Father," I said, falling to my knees beside him.

"Rowan?" His rheumy eyes searched for me in the darkness.

"Father, I'm here. I'm safe."

"Rowan. I am sorry for all the trouble I have brought you."

"It's all right," I said, fighting back tears. "I am safe. I am happy even, except to see you suffering."

"It's all my fault, child. All my fault. The rose . . . a rose for my Rowan, I thought, but . . ."

"You couldn't have known."

"Couldn't have known?" His voice hardened. "Everything I touch is damned. First your mother, then my ships, and then my daughter, all taken from me, all cursed, all gone."

"No." I squeezed his hand. "I'm here now. I forgive you, father."

"You look so much like your mother," he said, once again wandering into memory.

"She would want you to live. We all want you to live."

"Live. How can I live, without my Rowan?"

"I am here," I tried again, but he did not seem to hear me.

"The rose . . ." He broke into a fit of coughing.

The rose.

I placed my hand on my father's thin chest, feeling the rasp of his breathing, and spoke, my voice carrying echoes of a power rooted high up on the mountain. "I forgive you, father. I was angry at you once, but the Huntress was right. A rose for a rose, a thorn for a thorn, only it didn't mean what she thought it meant. You can't have a rose without thorns. It wouldn't be a rose. You can't have love without loss or happiness without sorrow, and I didn't understand that. You gave me that rose for a reason. The Huntress let you go for a reason."

The rose stirred in my hand, putting out vines.

"You gave me that rose because you wanted to make me happy, and you did. I was scared at first, and I missed you all so much, but I never belonged here. I found where I belong. It's with her. I know that's almost impossible to believe, but it's true. I love her, father. I love her in a way I could never have loved Avery. And she has so many books, and a library you can't even imagine, and I can shoot a bow and throw a spear now."

The tendrils spread over his chest, and Aspen gasped behind me.

"You didn't lose me, father. I forgive you, and you have to forgive yourself. We need you. Aspen needs you. She's going to have

179

a child soon. Don't you want to meet your grandchild? Juniper needs you. I need you." Tears rolled down my cheeks. "I learned something in the snow. Death is easy. Living is much, much harder, but I promise you this: if you let yourself die, you will miss out on so much that is beautiful."

A single, white rose bloomed, and the soft fragrance filled the room.

"Rowan?"

Aspen burst into tears at the sound of my father's voice, no longer threaded with madness.

"I'm here," I said. The rose lost its petals, one by one, the vine shriveling as the magic faded, its task complete.

"Rowan. I have missed you." He looked around the room, then down at his shrunken body. "I hardly know myself."

"It doesn't matter. We know you," said Aspen, squeezing his other hand.

"Seize her."

The command took the three of us by surprise, and I struggled against the arms that grabbed me, hauling me from the room and dragging me down a hallway. I was strong now from a year in the mountains, and I broke free long enough to catch a fist in my face and another in my ribs before I was thrown into a cold, dark pit that I recognized as the village jail before the door was shut and barred behind me.

"No," I screamed, beating my fists against the bars. Someone shoved a torch into my face, and I barely recognized Avery. His face was twisted with hatred, and his eyes blazed with dark intention. At his side stood the old woman.

"Tell her what you told me," he said, and I heard triumph in his voice.

"The curse is broken," she said.

"The curse?" Fear filled my mouth.

"The Huntress has lost her power."

"No." My voice barely rose above a whisper.

"She is weak," Avery said, and past him I noticed the mob, dressed for the mountains and armed to the teeth. "She is weak, and we will at last be rid of her. I shall avenge my father and my brother, and the wealth of the mountain will belong to us. Your father was right, Rowan. We will hunt her lands, and with the wealth of her furs we will prosper, and you will never look down on me again."

"Avery," I said, but the madness that had left my father had taken root in the man in front of me.

"I will kill the Huntress myself." His eyes bulged, and the crowd behind him cheered.

"Please, Avery," I begged.

He laughed in my face.

"You scorned me, Rowan, and you chose to love a monster over me. This is the price." He turned to face the crowd. "Who's with me?"

A hundred voices roared their approval, and I watched my sister's husband march off into the woods to kill the woman I loved.

"You'll never find her," I shouted after him.

A soft chuckle of laughter disagreed with me. "On the contrary, child. You've led them right to her."

The old woman had not followed the mob, and I craned my neck to see her through the bars.

"How?"

"The roses do not give up what is theirs so easily. They bloomed in your footsteps as you came down the mountain. Even a child could follow them."

"Why?" I asked her.

She gave me a piercing look. "Why what, child?"

"Why did you tell him?"

A smile flitted across her ancient face. "The same reason I cursed her."

I screamed a wordless cry of rage, lunging for her through the bars.

"Do you not want to know the reason?" she asked, stepping just beyond my reach.

"Because you are a bitter, evil old hag?" I guessed, still trying

181

to claw her face with my hands. Behind her, I saw the gleam of a pair of golden eyes, and I grinned, for the first time understanding how a person could murder another and enjoy it.

Kill her, I willed the pup.

The wolf pup sat at the witch's feet, tilting her head to stare at me as the witch answered.

"To save her."

The air left my lungs in a painful whoosh, and I hung from the door, panting. "How could a curse save her?"

"The woman I cursed was not worthy of your love, child. She was cruel and careless with the hearts and lives of others. A woman like that could not rule the mountains. A woman like that would have destroyed us all, and the loss would have meant nothing to her. So I condemned her to an eternity of winter, until she learned what it was like to lose one she loved more than her own life. It would seem that is you."

"She hasn't lost me."

"She thinks she has, and that is what matters. She believes she understands the curse, but she only sees what she fears."

"Tell me. Tell me the curse you placed on her."

"First, I must tell you a story."

"There isn't time. I have to stop Avery. I have to warn her."

"Once, a long time ago, there was a woman."

I closed my eyes, her voice overriding my panic as she told me the story the Huntress had revealed only in fragments, about a boy and a hunt and a woman who would have crushed her chiefdom beneath the heels of her boots if it pleased her.

"What will happen to her now?" I asked when it was over.

"That, child, is entirely up to you."

"What can I do against a mob of rabid villagers?"

"Do you love her?" The old woman's eyes were as bright as the wolf's.

"Yes."

"Then you will have to find a way."

She woke with her Hounds around her. Brendan, Masha, Neve, Lyon, and Quince, dressed for the hunt and laughing, bows and axes at their sides and blood on their clothes.

"The game is so much better in the lowlands," Masha was saying as the Huntress opened her eyes. "And their hunters are lazy. We should raid this spring."

"You always want to raid," said Neve, polishing the head of her axe. "Why raid when we could just hunt?"

"If we raid, they will be afraid. Then we can start tithing them for protection," said Lyon. "Game and grain. Think of how fat the horses will be."

"Think of how fat I will be." Brendan smacked his stomach. "What say you, Isolde?"

The Huntress looked at Quince, who had not yet spoken. There was something wrong with her face. She was grinning a wolf's grin and her teeth were too sharp.

"Quince," the Huntress said, but as she spoke her Hound faded, and where she had stood was the alpha female of the pack, her tongue lolling over ivory jaws. The wolf snarled once, then trotted out of the room.

"Wait," she called after her, but the wolf did not heed her, and the fire sputtered in the grate, casting strange shadows on the wall.

Chapter Twenty

Something wet and warm brushed my cheek. I pushed it away, thinking it was the wolf, and met resistance.

"Hush, Row," said a familiar voice.

I tried to open my eyes. One obeyed. The other was swollen shut, letting in only a sliver of light. My head throbbed with the sort of ominous intensity that promised to only get worse the longer I remained conscious, and so I closed my eyes again. The pup could wait to eat. She was almost fully grown, and she knew her way to the stables where there was always a carcass to be had.

"Rowan."

It was so like the Huntress to wake me when I wanted sleep most.

The Huntress.

Avery.

My good eye snapped open and Aspen stared back, holding a damp cloth in her hand and wearing an anguished expression.

"Aspen?" I said, my panic momentarily replaced by confusion.

"How are you feeling?" she asked.

"I have to go. I have to warn her."

Aspen looked over my head, and I turned, braving the new lance of pain that shot through my skull to see Juniper sitting on my other side. We were in a small room, decorated with rugs and sporting its very own washbasin. I squinted. I seemed to recall losing consciousness in the cold darkness of the jail, not the house.

"You can't," Aspen said, pressing the warm cloth to my face again. "You need to rest."

I pulled myself into a sitting position, then swore. It was not just my head that hurt. My chest felt as if it had been kicked by a horse.

"What happened to me?"

"You . . ." Aspen had an awed, almost reverent expression on her face. "You did not go quietly when Avery ordered you locked up. You don't remember?"

I shook my head, instantly regretting it.

"I was able to convince them to move you back in here once Avery left, but I think that's mostly because the villagers who didn't go with Avery felt a little guilty about what happened to you."

"I have to stop him."

"You'll never catch them, Row."

"Aspen." My sister flinched at my tone, and I saw her press her hand to her swollen belly. "Do you really think Avery can stop her?"

"The hedgewitch says she's weak."

"But what about her wolves? Her bear? Even weak, she's still a match for Avery."

"He won't be alone."

"And neither will she. I have to go."

"Or stay," Aspen pleaded. "Stay with us, help us with Father, and when this is over maybe you'll be free."

The rose inside me unfurled, spreading its petals wide. I would not be free. I would never be free again if Avery killed her.

"Love is like that. Beautiful, intoxicating even, but sharp as broken glass. You must handle it like you would a rose. Gently, knowing when to prune and when to water, and you must never grasp a cane too tightly, or it will cut you."

"You don't understand," I began, but Aspen cut me off.

"I do understand. This woman killed my husband's family and

stole my sister. She has you under some sort of spell, Rowan, and I will not let you go out there to die."

"You didn't exactly seem happy to see me."

"You don't know how you looked, standing there in the snow in these furs with that wolf at your side. I thought you were *her*. I thought that if Avery realized he had been wrong, he would go after her, and I would lose him too." She stopped, tears welling in her eyes. "I was right."

"Aspen," I said, placing my own hand on the swell of her womb. "If you love him. If you love me. If you want this child to have a father, then let me go."

"He told me to keep you here where you were safe."

"The Huntress will kill them. What if the witch is wrong? What if he is marching right into a trap? The witch told me the curse, and it isn't clear what happens to the Huntress once it's broken. It doesn't say anything about weakness." I took hope from my own words. "Even if one of them manages to put a spear in her, which I doubt, the rest will die. Her wolves will tear them to pieces, and her bear will break their bones like twigs. What they don't eat, the snow will bury, until the only thing left of the Locklands is the baby in your belly, and for all I know she might come for him too."

Aspen wrapped her arms around her middle. "And she'll listen to you?"

"She will."

"But Avery won't." Her eyes darkened with resolve. "I'll come with you."

"Aspen, you're pregnant. You can't be out there, and you don't know the woods like I do."

"I won't slow you down," said Juniper, speaking up for the first time. "Avery might not listen to me, but Bjorn will."

"Bjorn?" I asked.

"Her betrothed," said Aspen, looking thoughtful. "He is close with Avery, but he's nowhere near as pigheaded."

I hesitated. Juniper was only fourteen. Too young to be married, and way too young to be climbing these mountains. They had already claimed me and condemned my father. I couldn't put Juniper at risk.

"Besides," Juniper said, sounding smug, "you won't be moving as quickly as you'd like, what with a black eye and bruised ribs. You might need me."

"You could get hurt, or worse."

"If Avery dies, Bjorn dies too. I lose either way. Let me help."

I didn't have time to argue. Every second that passed brought Avery closer to the Huntress and, for all my words, it was not Avery I was worried about. The Huntress was only one woman, and there was an urgency to the whisper of the thorns that set my teeth on edge.

"We need to leave now."

"There's a problem," said Aspen, biting her lip. "Big Tom's guarding the door."

"Who's Big Tom?"

My sisters gave me a look of disgust so achingly familiar I nearly smiled.

"Did you pay attention to anything in this village?" Aspen asked.

"Or, you know, open your eyes?" Juniper shook her head at me. "Big Tom is the butcher's son, and he's about seven feet tall and built like an ox, only he's not dumb like one."

"So why didn't they take him with them?"

"He hurt his leg pretty badly a few weeks ago, but even with a limp he's still more than a match for the three of us."

"Juniper, can you get us some food and some warm clothing for yourself?"

"This is my room, so the clothing part is easy. I don't know about the food."

"Try. We'll only get one shot at this. I also need you to find out where they put my bow."

Juniper nodded.

"Now."

When the door shut behind her, I turned to Aspen.

"Are you going to kill Tom?" she asked me.

"No." I held a hand to my head to try to stop the ache. "Does he trust you, Aspen?"

"I don't know."

"Would he come if you called for help?"

"Yes."

"Good. Then do exactly as I tell you. And trust me."

Aspen's shriek would have sent me running if I'd heard it, and it worked on Big Tom. The door crashed in with a groan and a spray of splinters, followed by one of the largest men I had seen in my entire life. My hand spasmed on the knife I held to Aspen's throat, and she gave a very real whimper as it nicked her exposed skin.

"Stop right there, or she dies," I said in the best snarl I could manage, given that the sight of Big Tom's thick neck and bulging muscles had turned my legs to water.

"You wouldn't hurt your sister," Tom said, taking an impossibly long stride toward us.

I jerked the knife, forcing Aspen's head back.

"Stop," Aspen said in a croaking voice. "Please, Tom."

Tom paused, eyes darting back and forth between us.

"You're right, Tom," I said, trying to sound unbalanced. It wasn't as difficult as it should have been. "I won't kill her. But I'll hurt her. Badly. And then I'll call for my mistress, and whisper your name into the snow." He blanched. "Unless you let me go." I watched his face as he processed this, and felt a twinge of empathy. Tom looked like the sort of man who feared very little, thanks to his size, but magic was something else entirely.

"I can't," he said, steeling himself. "I can't let you go." There was a heaviness to his voice.

"Please, Tom," said Aspen.

"I can't let her send a warning."

"You idiot," I said, shoving Aspen away from me as roughly as I dared. Tom caught her, and in the moment of space that bought me I reached for him. The vines were ready. Tom screamed as they wrapped around his throat, and I ducked out of the room before anyone else came running.

Juniper waited in the hallway. She grabbed my hand and pulled me toward the back of the lodge. "There's another way out," she said, ducking through a smaller door that led directly out to the woodshed. "And now we have to run."

I clenched my jaw against the pain in my body and sprinted over the packed snow and into the trees.

The bear was gone.

Her hand slipped on the axe, and it bounced, nearly clipping her in the face as her body failed to compensate. She had blown her horn, calling the Hounds and the bear for the hunt, and the bear had not come.

Fish swam below.

She watched them, the axe forgotten as the lake ice bit into her knees.

The bear had come to her with the first snows, lumbering out of the drifts like something from another age. She remembered the feel of its fur, thick enough it nearly swallowed her arm to the elbow before she found the slab of muscle underneath.

Where it had come from or who it had been she had never known and never asked, not that the creature would have answered. It hadn't mattered. Unlike the wolves, the bear did not age and mate and whelp and die. She was like the Huntress—unchanging, elemental.

Gone.

A drop of water fell on the blade of her axe.

She closed her eyes, loosing another tear as the wind blew across the ice, bringing with it the smell of rain.

Chapter Twenty-One

Descending the mountain had been treacherous. Every exposed slope was an avalanche waiting to happen, and the cold stole in, weakening healthy muscles and promising peace and warmth and death.

Ascending was ten times harder.

Juniper was right about the bruised ribs. Every breath of frigid air hurt, and I had to lean on her from time to time to ease the ache. Soon, though, everything ached. The incline was relentless, and I had not eaten well since I had left the keep. Game was scarce outside the boundary. What little food Juniper had packed might have to last us days, and she had not had time to find my bow.

I missed the wolf. She had not returned, and I felt her absence like another ache. I also missed her jaws. Even a mouse or shrew would have been welcome.

Juniper looked like she felt little better than I did by the end of the first day. I might have been more bruise than muscle, but at least my body was used to navigating deep snow. What I could see of her face beneath her scarf was grim with determination, and she was more than happy to let me build the fire when darkness fell.

"How far?" she asked as I melted a little snow over the fire for us to drink.

"Far." I didn't have the energy to say more. We stared into the flames, too exhausted to sleep, and let feeling creep back into our fingers and toes.

"Why?" Juniper said just as I was nodding off.

"Why what?"

"Why did you wait so long to come home?"

"I was a prisoner, remember?"

"Aspen said you told father you belonged there."

I watched the fire, trying not to relive the memory of the Huntress turning away from me, the sweep of her shoulders hunched and broken. "You should sleep, Juniper."

She curled up against me, and I waited for her shivers to subside before I let myself drift off, checking and double-checking that the fire stayed lit.

I dreamed of a high mountain meadow, where a cool, earthy breeze swept up from the lowlands and meltwater trickled down from the peaks. In the center of the meadow stood a white horse. There was something vaguely familiar about it, and as I stared, dazzled by the sunlight, I saw the body at its hooves. I knew, with the certainty of dreams, that I had to get to that body, but my feet were tangled in a snarl of thorns, and they bit deeper with each step I took, ensnaring me further in the briars.

I woke in a cold sweat to add more branches to the fire. The wind had picked up in the night, and the flames guttered low even in the sheltered bowl I had scooped out for us from the drifts. Above, the stars burned with the peculiar brightness of early morning. I thought of how much brighter they would be from the top of the mountain, with the sweep of the lake beneath me and no fire to dim them, and bit back a sob.

The second day was harder than the first. The slopes were steeper here and the snow higher. Last night's wind had swept the drifts back into the trail broken by the Locklands, and we had to force our way through with none of the comparative ease of the day before. Each excruciatingly slow step heightened the growing sense of panic that had haunted me since last night's dream. We were not gaining on the Locklands. If anything, we were falling behind, and the roses straggling through the snow had a wilted, damaged look to them that suited my mood. I formed ice balls in half-frozen hands to throw at adventurous squirrels but missed each and every shot I took. Juniper's harsh, rasping breath pressed too loudly on my ears.

"Breathe through your nose," I told her, straining to hear anything beyond the sound.

"I can't. It's clogged."

I tried to bury my irritation and missed another shot at a squirrel. I did, however, find his cache of acorns, which looked like the worst of the tannins had been leeched out of them. Roasted nuts would give us strength.

"What are we going to do when we get there?"

I looked up from the meager meal I'd laid out to thaw before the fire. Juniper's eyes watched me expectantly, wide and dark and young.

"Try and talk Avery out of it," I said, looking away.

In truth, I had no idea what we were going to do if we caught up with Avery. I didn't think he would listen to me, and I didn't think Juniper's Bjorn would make much of a difference, either. The Huntress had laid most of Avery's family in the ground. I didn't see much hope for a peaceful resolution.

"You know that isn't going to work," Juniper said, calling my bluff.

"We have to try." I gave the fire an overly vicious stab.

"Do you have to save her?" She spoke in barely a whisper, but the accusation was loud and clear. An ugly silence descended. "Why?" She asked, finally. "Is it the magic?"

"No." An owl hooted in the distance. The sound emphasized the gulf between me and my sister, and I felt the miles of wilderness stretching out around us to either side.

"I don't understand. She kidnapped you. She *killed* people, Rowan."

"I know."

"Then why?" she asked again, her face incredulous.

A gust of wind tossed the pine boughs over our camp and dislodged a fine mist of snow. I raised my face to it, letting the cold burn against my cheeks and listening for the distant cry of wolves. The wind carried only its own howl, however, and did not blow away Juniper's words.

"I love her," I said, the sound of rustling rose leaves rising to a cacophony. "I love her, and I left her, and now everything is falling apart."

There was something wrong with the roses. I grew more certain of this with each passing day. My feet crunched on fallen petals, frozen into perfect, translucent shapes that bloomed the palest of pinks against the snow. Had they ever dropped their petals before? I could not remember. We should have neared the boundary by now, but all I saw were the roses that had followed me down.

Juniper trailed behind me, speaking only when necessary and watching me out of eyes that seemed to take up half her face. She was hungry and angry, and I held the blame for both. The bitter taste of resin and bark filled my mouth. Bitter, but better than nothing, and I knew we had to save the last of the bread and sausage in her bag for the return.

"You should go back," I told her again, pausing to let us catch our breath. "You have enough food to get you home if you follow the hedge, and it will be easier going downhill."

She shook her head.

"Please, Juniper. You'll be safer there."

"You were screaming in your sleep last night," she said, surprising me.

The dreams of spring came every night now, and every night I failed to reach the body in the meadow.

"I'm sorry for waking you."

Juniper shrugged, then pushed past me.

"Catch your breath," I warned her. "You'll need it."

Ahead of us rose a forbidding stretch of white wasteland that I remembered from my descent. Far up it, clinging to the white like little black ants, struggled a line of tiny figures. I knew from my time with the Huntress that distances in the mountains were deceiving. Avery and the rest of the villagers could be a day ahead of us or more. They had the luxury of taking turns breaking trail, and more food besides. I squinted. They were moving carefully, and with good reason. It was no coincidence that I remembered that stretch.

"Look." I pointed, and Juniper followed the line of my hand in time to see a wall of white break away from the cliff, sending up a cloud of snow and setting off a rumble that we could hear from here. The figures were far enough away to escape unharmed, but an avalanche was a bad sign. If one part of the slope was unsteady, the rest could be, too, and half a mountain of snow had just filled the small valley between us and the trail. Juniper took a step toward me, forgetting her anger in fear.

"Are we safe here?" she asked. Plumes of snow were still rising into the sky.

"We're not safe anywhere out here. That's why you should go home. I shouldn't have let you come."

"You don't get to *let* me do anything."

"We're never going to catch up with them in time. Go back and tell Aspen we failed."

"No."

"You know what we'll find if we're too late, don't you?" I asked her. "Death. You don't know what she's capable of. What her beasts are capable of."

"Or maybe we'll find her body, and the bodies of her beasts. You don't know what the Locklands are capable of, either."

I flinched at the cold fury in her voice, and at the images her words conjured.

"Or we'll be lost out here and die of cold and hunger," I said. "We'll have to go miles out of our way now, and we could lose their trail entirely. Nobody will find our bodies, I promise you that, except the crows and foxes."

"You should never have come home." Her words echoed Aspen's.

"You're right. It was so stupid of me to want to save my father.

196

I'm a terrible, terrible person for daring to think that I could bring one bit of good into this goddamned awful world."

"Go on. Feel sorry for yourself. I tried that for a while too after you were taken prisoner." Juniper crossed her arms over her chest, sneering the last word.

"I *was* a prisoner."

"Were you? Then why are you running back to your jailer?"

"Because life isn't simple, Juniper. Shouldn't you have figured that out by now? Marriage isn't simple. Love isn't simple, no matter what Bjorn may have told you."

"You don't get to talk about Bjorn. You want them all dead."

"I don't want anybody dead. That's the point. I don't want Avery to kill the Huntress, and I don't want the Huntress to kill Avery. I don't belong in that village, Juniper, but that doesn't mean I hate them."

"You never even tried to belong."

"I was the price father was willing to pay for *your* belonging. We're merchant's daughters. That means we're goods, whether we want to be or not. Look at me, Juniper. I never wanted to marry Avery. You know that. He knew that. But Aspen loves him. Who knows? She might find happiness once this is all over, which is something I could never have done with Avery. I didn't mean to fall in love with the Huntress. I didn't mean to be happy. I didn't want to wake up one day and realize that the only time in my life I have ever really felt free was when I was trapped in an enchanted castle."

"But what about us?" Juniper's lower lip quivered.

"I missed you every day, Juniper, and if I could have gotten a message to you, I would have. None of this is fair. I wish we didn't have to make these choices, and now . . ." I trailed off, looking up at the broken slope with barely suppressed panic. "Now I'm too late."

The shadows on the snow lengthened. The sky had gone from cold blue to a colder pink as we fought, and now the wind rose, carrying with it a mournful howl that I almost recognized.

Juniper placed a mittened hand in mine. "We can still make

197

another mile before nightfall," she said. "Two, maybe, if we're lucky."

I nodded and squeezed her fingers, turning away so that she did not see the tears of frustration freezing on my cheeks.

A branch cracked. Both Juniper and I started, and I reached for my bow before I remembered I'd lost it. The shadows beneath the pines were blacker than night. One detached itself from the trees and loped toward us, and my heart nearly leapt from my throat before I recognized the gleam of eye and teeth. The wolf paused a few feet away, eyeing us. I dropped to my knees, begging her to come to me with open hands. Instead, she looked over her shoulder. Another shape emerged from the shadows, and then another.

"Rowan?" Juniper asked in a shaky voice.

"It's okay," I told her, counting off the members of the pack. Almost all were here. My heart rose again, this time in hope, and I strained my eyes toward the trees for more signs of movement. *There.*

Her white fur caught the light, and the huge white bear lumbered soundlessly into view on giant paws. She was riderless.

"Where is she?" I asked the pack. My voice cracked on the last word. "Where is she?"

The wind picked up, empty and cold and damp. Snow was coming. We were out of time.

"What's going on, Rowan?"

I didn't answer. The pack never roamed outside the boundary without the Huntress. I hadn't thought they could. My skin prickled in fear. "Juniper, you're not going to like this," I told her, and then I dragged her with me to the bear.

Her muzzle swung toward me. I had forgotten in the days I had been gone just how much the bear stank. This close, it was nearly overpowering, and I blinked fresh tears from my eyes. The smell would lessen once we were on top. I let the bear sniff me, and then I placed a hand on her shoulder, hoping she would understand. I was too weak to clamber up without help.

The bear knelt.

Juniper whimpered as I heaved myself across the bear's shoulders, and she went boneless with panic as I hauled her up after me. "Hold on," I warned, and then the forest slid away as the familiar gait of the animal carried us off into the trees.

Only the alpha female stayed.

The Huntress stroked her fur, resting her cheek against the cold of the stone.

It was raining again, and though the rain froze when it hit the walls of the keep, it was still rain.

A thousand years ago, it seemed, she had raised her face to the first spring rains, listening to the groan of the lake ice breaking up, waiting for the first of the ferns to uncurl near the shadows where the snow still lingered.

Or perhaps she dreamt the rain.

It was strange, this weakness. This cold.

She had never been weak.

She had never had cause to doubt her body, not since she had been a child, struck with fever.

Her hand paused on the wolf's hip.

Perhaps all this had been a fever dream. The Hunt. The bear. The ice, the snow, and Rowan.

No.

Rowan was real.

She saw her now as she had seen her last, on her knees in the snow, anguish on her face. The Huntress had been able to ease that pain.

"I am a fool," she whispered to the wolf. "I should have kept her here. I should have told her the price she would pay for her father's life."

The smell of roses was suffocating.

"I am so sick of roses," she said, the effort of speaking almost more than she could stand.

What she would give to see a different flower. What she would give, still, to lay Rowan down in a field of budding clover, with the sun hot and high above them as she lifted Rowan's shirt and kissed the soft curve of her stomach, the breeze soft and gentle and free of any memory of ice. What she would give for another life.

Chapter Twenty-Two

Night fell. The bear ran, tireless and silent, through the thinly treed upper slopes. Juniper nodded off behind me, her arms wrapped around my waist and her head lolling against my back while I tightened shaking legs around the bear's withers. My eyes burned with cold and exhaustion, but the bear showed no sign of stopping, and neither did the wolves.

Snow swirled around us. It was thick and heavy, the kind of snow that melts and soaks through clothing before accumulating, and water dripped off the front of my hood before freezing into long, thin icicles that clinked together as we rode on. The bear took us away from the avalanche's path, down narrow gullies and along high ridges spotted with rock. My eyes adjusted to the starless night slowly, and I saw the world in a haze of black and gray and cold.

Cold. There were not enough words for cold in our language, the Huntress had told me. She had a book in her library that claimed the people of the northern wastes had a hundred words for snow alone, and we had spent an afternoon trying to come up with our own language.

"We need a word for the kind of cold that splits trees in two," she'd said.

"And the cold that doesn't feel cold at first, until you've been out in it too long and your hands and feet and lips stop working," I had said, shivering.

She'd kissed me.

"Your lips still seem to be working."

"Do you even feel the cold?" I'd asked, watching a gust of wind blow snow across her cheek.

"Sometimes."

Now, as an icy finger snaked inside my hood and down my neck, I realized we'd forgotten one: the kind of cold that slipped inside the heart, one part winter, two parts fear, a cold that froze the blood with creeping terror until even the mountains shrank beneath the weight of the ice inside me. *Faster,* I urged the bear.

I slept somehow as night stretched into morning. The lumbering stride never faltered beneath me, and the bear shifted her weight to catch me each time I threatened to slide off. Juniper cried with exhaustion and fear. Her sobs matched the rhythm of the bear's stride, then subsided, and we ate the sausage and bread we'd been saving for the journey home. We both seemed to know that no matter what we found at the end of our ride, a few bits of blood sausage and brown bread would not make one bit of difference.

"Rowan."

I closed my eyes and listened to the Huntress's voice rise out of my memory, more real than the daylight around me.

"You look like your wolf," she'd told me the morning after we'd lain together for the first time.

I had stared up at her, my limbs still tangled in hers and my body heavy with sleep, awed into silence by the magnitude of the change that had grown within me at her touch. Even the weak winter sunlight felt different. Brighter somehow, and yet less solid.

"You belong here. You're wild, in your own way."

I had thought of my city, with its comfortingly familiar maze of streets, and the sharp stench of sewage and spices and overripe bodies pressed close against the sea. That was where I had thought I belonged, but cold stripped away illusion. Sinew and bone and fire were all that mattered, and there was comfort there in the space between life and frozen death. Comfort, and purpose, and a freedom as fierce as winter's fury.

"Rowan."

The voice was wrong. I jolted awake as Juniper shook my shoulder, and the world slid back into focus. Before us stretched the lake. The bear paused on the shore, breathing out huge clouds of steam. Her muscles trembled beneath us, and I wondered what the journey had cost her.

Home, rustled the rose.

"Let's go," I said to the bear, but she remained poised on the edge, weaving her snout back and forth. One of the wolves trotted out over the ice, and then he too paused, sniffing the frozen surface. He returned to the pack with an odd, careful gait, and then Juniper's gasp brought my attention to the line of figures struggling across farther down the shore.

"There's still time," she said.

"Go," I told the bear, digging my heels into her ribs. She roared in response, rising on her haunches, and Juniper and I tumbled off into the snow. When I pushed myself to my feet, my legs weak and aching from the endless ride, the bear had loped off around the edge of the lake, avoiding the ice entirely.

"No," I shouted after her. "Come back."

"Look." Juniper knelt at the edge, clearing the snow away from the surface. I crouched beside her, and my heart stopped with fear. Hairline fractures crisscrossed the surface, white against the thick black ice.

"That's impossible," I said, looking around me at the snow and the high cold sky. The lake never thawed.

"Do you think we're light enough to make it across?" Juniper asked.

I glanced at the wolves. They had not followed the bear, and were watching me expectantly. Some of them weighed as much as I did, but they had four paws to distribute their weight, where we had only two feet. Going around would be safer, but it would add miles to our journey, and Avery was already a quarter of the way across.

"Follow me, but stay at least three meters behind," I said, putting one foot on the ice. It held. My pup trotted out ahead of me with her nose to the ground, following a trail of her own. I took a deep breath to steady my nerves and followed.

Each step brought us closer to the castle on the far shore, and each step took us farther away from safety. I knew nothing about ice. No thaw had come to this mountain in living memory from what I could tell, and the Huntress had not spoken of the time before. The snow on the lake made it nearly impossible to judge the appearance of the surface. Even so, I could tell the difference underneath my feet. Some places were as hard and impenetrable as I remembered. Others had a soft, yielding quality that turned my stomach. In a few places, water filled my footsteps, and I prayed to whatever gods were listening that the ice would hold.

We heard the screams when we were halfway across, and heard the unmistakable crack of breaking ice. I dropped to my knees, thinking to spread my weight, but Juniper started to run toward the Locklands.

"No," I shouted after her, and then I was running, scrambling to grab her as her foot sank through a rotten patch and she teetered, arms flailing, standing at the edge of the river of meltwater that snaked its way across the lake and separated us from the Locklands.

"I've got you," I told her, hauling her back onto safer ground. She kept screaming, and I followed her line of sight, horror welling in my throat.

Several of the villagers were in the water. I could see the small dark shapes of their heads, and heard the shouts of the rest of them as ropes were thrown and lines formed to pull the freezing men and women from the black water of the lake.

I closed my eyes. Even if they got them out of the water, they were dead if they didn't get warm. I forced Juniper into a sitting position and pulled her boot off her foot. She was lucky. The water had not soaked through, and the boot was already freezing over. I helped her get it back on, and she looked up at me with dull eyes.

"What if that was Bjorn?"

"It wasn't," I told her, willing myself not to let my voice shake. I hoped, for Juniper's sake, that it hadn't been her boy, but it had been someone. "We have to go. Be even more careful. If you feel the ice start to break, go back, not forward, and if we get separated follow our trail back to shore. Don't think about Bjorn," I added as her eyes strayed back towards the villagers. "We need to focus."

The far shore was a just few yards away when the wolf yipped out her warning, leaping sideways as a great chunk of ice tilted up under my weight, nearly dislodging her and sending me plunging into the lake. Cold exploded against my lungs. It knocked the breath from my body and sent stars shooting across my vision. Juniper's screams echoed strangely, and then my breath returned, blocking out all other sound in great, shuddering gasps that failed to mobilize my limbs. The ice shelf floated a few inches from my face, and from here I could see the striations and bubbles within the candled ice. This wasn't something that had happened overnight. This was a thaw that had been a long time in coming, and in that cold, dark, space of water, I finally understood.

The cold.

The roses.

The horse in the meadow and the briars and the thorns that still pierced my heart. They were a language, just like my mother had told me so many years ago in the warmth of her summer garden. Juniper screamed my name again, but the sound was far away. I saw, through the rotten ice, a hundred years of cold. I saw a young woman astride a snow white mare, cantering through a forest green with the first leaves of spring and white with the last rime of frost, a pack of leggy wolfhounds at her heels, and I saw an old woman walking to meet her, snow filling up her footsteps. She turned to look at me through the ice. Wrinkles grazed her lips and folded her eyes, tiny lines that spread like the cracks in the ice, but the eyes beneath them were familiar.

Rowan, said the witch, and water rushed into my mouth as I tried to answer.

"Rowan. Rowan!" A hand seized my hood, pulling me back

towards the surface. Juniper lay flat on her belly, arms outstretched, while my wolf stood beside her with anxious eyes.

There's still time, said the old voice, still strong, a memory trapped in ice like the Huntress's fish, swimming free into the clear, cold spring at last. I reached for Juniper and the rose unfurled, leaves and vines and thorns lashing themselves onto the porous surface of the lake and pulling me in with Juniper's help until we were panting and shivering on the shore.

The black gates rose before us. I traced the iron roses with my eyes, my body collapsing into paroxysms of cold.

"Come on," said Juniper.

I let her pull me to my feet, one arm around her shoulder, the other trembling along the wolf's back.

"T-t-t-this w-w-w-way." I stuttered the words between chattering teeth. The shadow of the stable fell over us, and I stumbled over bones and dried leaves on numb feet. Two more wolves detached themselves from the empty stalls. Juniper didn't whimper, and I didn't have the strength or coordination to reassure her, anyway. The stable opened into the abandoned hall. In the delirium of hypothermia, I thought I saw banners flapping from the rafters and smelled the rich aromas of roasting boar and frothing ale. Faces passed before me, people I had never met, ghosts, maybe, but real and warm and laughing. A few raised their mugs towards me, ale and mead and wine sloshing down the sides to pool on the floor where eager dogs snarled. I tried to smile back with frozen cheeks.

Ghosts followed us into the kitchen. A large woman stepped out of our way, bearing a tray of sweet breads, and a child tried to pluck one while her attention was elsewhere. A lithe woman with hair so blonde it was nearly white slapped the child's hand, then snatched a roll for herself with a wink at the cook. Fresh herbs and apples polished until they hurt the eye rested on platters. My mouth watered, and the heat from the many hearths burned against my face. Juniper sat me down before one, her face pinched with fear.

"It's okay," I tried to tell her, but no words came out.

Rowan.

The people in the kitchen paused, as if they, too, heard the woman's voice, and I watched in dismay as they faded away, leaving behind empty tables and dark hearths. Beside me, Juniper struggled to light the fire. I tried to help, but all I could do was shiver. "There," she said, catching a spark at last.

"Clothes," I managed to mumble. I had to get out of my wet clothes. Juniper nodded, and I noticed with detached clarity, as my sister peeled layer after layer of icy furs from my body until I was naked before the blaze, that a layer of dust had settled over the room.

I soaked up the warmth with my knees pulled up to my chest, staring into the fire as the delirium passed. The villagers who had shared my fate would not be so lucky. I could only hope that they had had the sense to light a fire when they got to the far shore. When the worst of the shivering retreated back into my marrow, I stood. My bare feet felt like ice against the flagstones.

"Go," I told Juniper. "Find Avery. Find Bjorn. Tell them there is fire and shelter here, if they leave their weapons behind. Tell them that if they do not, they will find only death."

"I can't leave you."

"Then stay here, by the fire, and warm yourself. There is food, somewhere. Rest. But I have to do the rest of this alone."

"Rowan—"

"Trust me."

"Take my cloak, at least," she said, unfastening it from her shoulders.

Juniper's hair was tangled and matted, as I was sure mine was too, and she looked less real than the ghosts I still could half see out of the corner of my eye. I did not wait to discover what Juniper decided. Time was running out. I could almost hear the sand running through the hourglass, only instead of sand, I heard the soft flutter of falling petals.

Her breath slowed.

Thought was no longer reliable.

Words, faces, half-formed memories of a world that once had been. They floated around her, and once she thought she stood on top of the mountain, stars surrounding her, close enough to touch in the soft darkness of the sky.

I was Winter once, she thought in a rare moment of clarity.

She did not know what she was now.

Sometimes, when the wolf turned to nose her gently, she thought she heard the howls of the rest of the pack, but not often.

How long have I been cold? she wondered. How many lifetimes have I spent frozen while the rest of the world turned?

She could feel the burden of all those years now, pulling her down into the stone. All that kept her alive was the magic that still lingered in the roses, and that too was dying.

Rowan, she tried to say, but her lips refused to move, and the wolf whined deep in her throat.

You are free now, she thought, looking into those golden eyes. Free to be what you have always been.

Chapter Twenty-Three

The halls were empty. My wolf paced beside me, sniffing at the cobwebbed corners, and I broke into as much of a run as my aching joints could manage.

"Where is she?" I asked the wolf as I tried to think. My mind was still fogged with cold and sluggish, but the answer rose out of that blank wasteland unbidden: the room at the top of the tower. The room that had remained locked throughout my entire stay, no matter how many times I asked the Huntress what was behind its door.

I ran.

The stairs went on and on and on. I crawled toward the end, my nails digging into the stone while the last of the dying briars whispered around me. *Too late,* they said, petals of ice melting on the steps as I came at last to the locked door. I pounded on it, the jolt sending spikes of pain up my arm and into my shoulder. There was no answer from the other side, but I could smell the cloying scent of decaying flowers.

The rose.

I pressed my palm against the iron, and the sound of the lock tumbling into place as a tendril of vines tripped it was the most beautiful thing I had ever heard.

No carpet graced the floor of the room beyond the door, and no tapestries adorned the walls. Instead, the entire room was hung with vines, and the floor was thick with drying petals. In the center, curled around each other like a pair of nesting birds, lay the Huntress and the alpha female of the pack. The wolf raised her head when I entered.

"No." I fell to my knees beside the Huntress and placed a hand on her shoulder. It was cold to the touch through the wool of her shirt, as was her cheek, and her chest rose and fell with the barest hint of life. "No," I said again, louder this time, and the sound went on and on, pouring out of the open window and over the lake where Avery and his armed mob waited to kill the woman who lay, nearly dead already, in a flood of roses. She did not move. I lifted her shoulders into my lap, cradling her head in my arms, and stroked her thick dark hair. "No. You can't leave me."

Her lips were pale and cold. I kissed them anyway, willing life back into her body. Nothing happened.

Shouts echoed from somewhere within the castle, and I heard the heart-stopping roar of the bear. Avery had arrived. I didn't care. The only thing that mattered was that the Huntress was dying.

"Rowan?" Her eyelids fluttered open, the green of her irises like a slice of spring.

"I'm here," I said, my voice breaking.

She raised a hand to touch my face.

"You came back." Her voice was clear, like running water, but faint.

"Of course. Did you doubt it?"

Her smile broke my heart all over again.

"I was always cursed to lose you."

"She believes she understands the curse, but she only sees what she fears," the witch had said.

"You're wrong," I told the Huntress. "Can't you see that? I'm here. I'm right here, Isolde."

"Are you?" Her eyes searched my face. "I've seen too many ghosts since you left."

"Tell me what to do. Tell me how to save you."

"Hunt. Remember me when the first green comes. Watch the first spring fawns. Listen to the birds." She turned her head to the

213

window. "Smell the damp soil on the breeze and walk through fens still cool with snow. Feel the sun warm the rocks in the high passes, where the mountain lions den and the eagles nest. Look down on the valleys and you'll understand. We were the eagles. We were the lions. We fell on them because they were below us, so far down they didn't even look real. She was right perhaps to curse me for that, but you should have seen us, Rowan. We were wild. We were . . ." She shuddered again, and I held her closer. "We were wrong. All flesh, all blood, all teeth and bone and grace."

"It's in the past now," I said.

"The past is everything."

"I'm here. Don't you see? That means you didn't lose me. That means there is still a future, and nothing in the curse said you have to die for your sins!"

"Don't leave me."

"I won't." The tears came faster now. "Just tell me how to save you."

"You already did." Her breath caught, and I held mine until she breathed again. "I love you. I loved you from the moment I saw you, even though I knew it meant this. You're worth a thousand springs."

"You can't die," I commanded her.

"I am the winter rose," she said. "And the roses are dying." Her face tightened with pain, and she turned her head away from me. Another shudder shook her, and this one lasted longer than the others. The room spun as I remembered the feel of thorns spreading in my veins.

"Wait," I said. "Wait. You can't leave me. I came back."

Footsteps pounded on the stairs and the white wolf rose, hackles up. I ignored her. It didn't matter. The Huntress's heart stuttered underneath my hand, flickering, fading, gone.

Snarls echoed against the stone, followed by screams.

"Stand aside," said Avery Lockland.

I looked up from her body through eyes blurred with tears. Avery stood in the doorway with blood seeping through his

214

clothes and briar scratches on his face, a bloody hatchet in each hand. I did not see my wolf.

"Move, Rowan."

I shook my head. I was waiting for the reassuring thud of a heart against ribs, and it wasn't coming. Avery took another step, his eyes flicking around the rose-strewn room. Then he saw the woman in my arms, and he froze.

"It doesn't matter anymore," I said.

"She's dead?" Disappointment twisted his face. "She can't be dead. She was mine to kill."

"Go," I told him. "Go back to your village before you kill any more of your neighbors. Go back to my sister and your child. Treat them well, Avery Lockland, or I will rip your throat out with my teeth."

Avery laughed. There was blood in his beard.

"You? You can't hurt me if she's dead. Step aside, Rowan. I'm going to bring her head back and mount it on my wall, right next to her wolves and that thrice damned beast of a bear." He raised an axe as he spoke, his eyes narrowing, and struck me across the face with the butt. I flew backward, skidding through the roses, until I lay with my face on the cool ground. The room tilted, then righted. Avery raised his axe again. He did not see the white she-wolf behind him, but I did, and I cried out as his downward swing missed the Huntress and took the wolf in the side, but not before her jaws closed on his arm. The crack of breaking bone split my ears, and Avery screamed.

The wolf growled, once, but then her jaw slackened, and she slid to the ground with his axe buried deep in her rib cage. Her eyes found mine. I held them, gold and black, huge as harvest moons, until they glazed over with death and the sound of Avery's ragged breathing filled the air. I pushed myself up to stand unsteadily on legs that desperately wanted to fold beneath me.

Avery let his broken right arm fall and raised his left. The blade glinted in the light from the window, arcing high above his head.

"No." The voice was mine, exploding from my chest, but the words were not. "You will not strike that blow, Avery Lockland."

Avery froze. I would have frozen, too, except my lips kept moving.

"It is done. The price has been paid. Your debt is settled. Go back to your greening hills and leave this place."

"I will leave. With her head."

"You will leave, and if you are lucky, you will get to take your own head with you."

"Who are you to threaten me, girl?"

I walked towards him, each step shaking but certain. "I am Winter, boy, and I will slaughter you like a spring lamb." A gust of wind rushed through the window, stirring up small whirlwinds of rose petals. They settled on the Huntress's body like a shroud. With the wind came a smell that made my chest ache anew. Rain. A clap of thunder shook the tower, but within me ice hardened, the power that had sustained the Huntress through her endless winter flooding into me.

"Rowan?" His arm shook with the effort of holding the axe and beads of sweat dripped down his face.

"Walk away, Avery Lockland."

He brought the axe down. Time slowed, frost blooming over my skin while rain began to fall outside the window. The Huntress lay between us, her face turned toward the rain and her dark hair spilling over the roses like black blood. Around her the briars stirred. Thorns rustled against each other as the vines shot across the floor, climbing up Avery Lockland's legs and sinking into his flesh. The axe fell from his hands and bounced harmlessly off the flagstones as blood streamed from a hundred punctures. When the thorns reached his throat and face, he screamed. I left him there. He would live, which was more than I could say for the wolf at his feet, but I did not believe in vengeance anymore. Nothing undid death.

I crawled to the Huntress, collapsing beside her. "You said you put a curse on her to save her," I said to the witch, wherever she was. "How is this salvation?"

"Poor child." The witch's voice rumbled with the strength of mountains. I did not look up. I heard her stoop to place a hand on Avery, and his ragged breathing calmed beneath her touch. "I had to know if she could ever love, and the surest way to measure love is loss."

"No," I said, resting my head against the Huntress's cool cheek. "There are other ways. You could have just asked me."

"She was willing to give up everything for you." The witch's words fell on my ears like a whisper of frost.

"And now you've taken everything from *me*."

"Have I?" She knelt on the Huntress's other side and placed a gnarled hand on her breast. "This is not death, child. She is merely feeling her mortality. She may yet die, though, without your help."

"I'll do anything."

"Would you give up your own life?"

I looked up into her eyes, and what I saw there was colder than the water of the lake. "Yes."

The witch considered this. "You would not be the first to die for her," she said.

"I don't care."

"She would never forgive you for making such a choice."

"*I don't care*," I said, the words turning into a shout.

"But I do not want your life, child." The witch smiled to herself as if this should have been obvious. "A rose for a rose, a thorn for a thorn. Haven't you been paying attention?"

Understanding blossomed before me.

I placed my hand on the Huntress's chest as I had done to my father, only this time I did not send out vines. The Huntress's back arched as the thorn pierced her heart, and I felt the whisper of the leaves rise into a storm that broke over me in a torrent of white-hot pain as the rose left me to take root in the Huntress's breast. I collapsed beside her, my hand sliding onto the hard ground, empty, with not so much as a scar to mark where the magic had been.

"Where the winter rose takes root, it grows, and its blossoming will mark the end of everything that you now hold dear," the witch said, patting the Huntress on the shoulder. "That is what I told her, but people never pay attention to semantics. What she held dear then was power and her own arrogance, things she could not hold onto and still love you." She rose, her joints creaking. "It gets tiring, always being right, in the end. But you see? I gave her the means to save herself, and perhaps her kingdom, if she still wants it."

"She might have learned that on her own."

"She might have, at great, great cost to others."

"What about her Hounds?" I asked, my eyes straying to the dead wolf. "You punished them for her crimes."

"That was part of the price she paid for power. They do not seem to have minded too much, however."

My wolf limped into the room as she finished speaking and lay down against my back to lick her wounds. "Who are you?" I asked, at last, feeling the Huntress's chest rising and falling slowly beside me.

"I am just an old, old woman." The witch picked up one of the faded petals and held it between two fingers. "But perhaps now I will become something else."

The petal fell, and I blinked. Where the witch had stood, I saw a young woman, with hair as fine and black as silk.

My jaw fell open.

"There is a king on the other side of these mountains in need of a lesson," she said, and I heard the memory of a cackle in her lilting voice.

Then she was gone.

"Rowan?" The Huntress stirred. She looked just as she had before, only less bright somehow and more real. Her eyes remained the same piercing green, but they were human—human and alive and full of wonder. I burst into tears, unable to speak.

"I don't understand." She held her hands up to the gray light. A bolt of lightning flickered outside.

I stopped trying to speak and flung myself on top of her, letting her arms wrap around me while I tangled my hands in her hair and pressed my lips to her cheek, then her neck, her collarbone, and the spot between her breasts where a single red rosebud lay, already fading. The sound of her beating heart filled my ears, and she tilted my face up to hers and kissed me hard. The world faded to a small round room at the top of a tower, where spring had come at last.

Epilogue

They say the winter rose still blooms, up there on the highest slopes, where the winter storms scour ice and snow into the shapes of beasts and the tops of the mountains scrape the stars. Some say the Huntress died that day. Others say that she lives on, stalking the snows as she always has, looking for the lost, the unwary, and the bold alike, and that the stories that came down from the mountains that spring were what they've always been: stories.

This is what I say. I say the Huntress still rides out, but her horn no longer calls ice down from the cold high places, and the briars that surround her keep no longer bloom in the snow. I say that her halls are no longer dark and empty, but filled with life and laughter, and that the only magic that still lingers is so old we've forgotten that it is magic at all.

I would know.

Avery had a change of heart once he woke from whatever spell the witch had placed on him. Perhaps he understood, at last, that we were not responsible for the choices of our fathers, or, more likely, he never quite forgot how near he came to death at my hands at the top of that tower. He returned to Aspen, and their child was born that spring, a blue-eyed, red-faced, squalling baby boy.

My father shed years like old rags when Aspen laid his grand-son in his arms. This turned out to be both blessing and curse, for as soon as he recovered his strength and wits he approached me with a plan. Surely the Huntress, now that she was freed from the clutches of a curse, would be interested in opening a line of trade. The furs she could bring from the upper slopes would fetch a fortune in the city, and now that she was mortal, she would need an income. Perhaps a marriage, too, could be arranged, both for myself and for the Huntress. My father knew many wealthy men.

She did not kill him, and neither did I, but he did not suggest marriage or furs again.

A few of the wolves stayed past the breaking of her power. The bear did not, and the Huntress watched her leave with a faraway look that I tried not to take personally, just as I learned to respect her occasional silences, and to expect that some mornings I would wake alone to find her gone, sometimes for a few hours, other times for a few days, and once or twice in the coldest months for weeks on end. There are different kinds of freedom. Each has its price.

The seasons passed. My pup grew gray hairs. The Huntress complained, every so often, of mortal maladies, her voice laden with indignation, and one summer I awoke in the middle of the night to a harvest moon so large it threatened to break open upon the peaks like a giant egg.

I slipped out of the keep and down to the shores of the lake to watch the moonlight spill out over the water. Footsteps, light and sure, followed me some time later, and neither the Huntress nor I spoke as she sat on the rocky shore beside me. I leaned my head against her shoulder and felt the certainty of happiness like a mortal wound. It was almost too much to bear, and yet we sat there, silent, two wild things caught in a moment of stillness that stretched out over the water like a held breath.

I say this, too.

Winter misses her. There is an agony to the way the winds howl around the keep in the darkness of the year. I think sometimes of the story of the winter rose, and I can almost believe it to be true. As for the Huntress, for all her longing for spring, for all that she loves me and I love her, there is an emptiness that will never leave her, a loss that runs as deep as the roots of these mountains. Sometimes I feel it too. Sometimes I think that there is a part of me that will always be frozen, a shard of ice lodged in my heart where a thorn used to be that a thousand, thousand summers will not melt.

A rose for a rose, a thorn for a thorn.

Acknowledgments

This is a fairy tale. Specifically, it is a loose retelling of *Beauty and the Beast*, and a great many talented writers have been here before me. I read as many retellings as I could under the guise of research for this book, and what I found gave me hope. In almost all of these retellings, it was not beauty that defined Beauty, but bravery. So here's to strong heroines, the writers who write them, and bravery in all its forms.

Much deserved thanks go out to the crew at Bywater Books for bringing *Thorn* together, and to Ann McMan, mentor and graphic designer extraordinaire. I am also lucky to have three phenomenal readers who are also exceptionally talented individuals in their own rights. Alessandra Amin, Stefani Deoul, and Karelia Stetz-Waters, as usual you rock.

Every writer needs a getaway. A big thank you to my grandmother for making so much possible and for providing all the wine, cheese, and ocean sunsets a writer could ask for.

In my naiveté, I actually thought this was going to be an easier book to write than my first. My wife chose the title as a tribute to my folly, and I confess I owe her an apology since what started out as a short story for her grew legs, ran away, and came back dressed up as a novel instead.

About the Author

ANNA BURKE graduated from Smith College with degrees in English Literature and Studio Art. She was the inaugural recipient of the Sandra Moran Scholarship for the Golden Crown Literary Society's Writing Academy and is currently pursuing an MFA in Creative Writing at Emerson College. Anna's debut novel, *Compass Rose*, was written while living on a small island in the West Indies, but *Thorn* is the byproduct of a long, cold New England winter. She currently lives in Massachusetts with her wife and their two dogs. You can learn more about her at www.annahburke.com.

COMPASS ROSE

**In the year 2513, the only thing higher than the seas
is what's at stake for those who sail them.**

Rose was born facing due north, with an inherent perception of cardinal points flowing through her veins. Her uncanny sense of direction earns her a coveted job within the Archipelago Fleet, but it also attracts the attention of Admiral Comita, who sends her on a secret mission deep into pirate territory.

Aboard the mercenary ship, Man o' War, Rose joins a ragtag crew under the command of Miranda, a captain as alluring as she is bloodthirsty. Rose quickly learns that trusting the wrong person could get her killed—and Miranda's crew have no desire to make anything easy for her. If Rose is going to survive the mission, she's going to have to learn to navigate more than ruthless pirates, jealous crewmates, swarms of deadly jellyfish, and a host of other underwater perils. Above all, she's going to need a strategy to resist Miranda's magnetic pull.

Compass Rose
Paperback   978-1-61294-119-6
eBook   978-1-61294-120-2

www.bywaterbooks.com

Bywater BOOKS

At Bywater Books we love good books about lesbians just like you do, and we're committed to bringing the best of contemporary lesbian writing to our avid readers. Our editorial team is dedicated to finding and developing outstanding writers who create books you won't want to put down.

We sponsor the Bywater Prize for Fiction to help with this quest. Each prize winner receives $1,000 and publication of their novel. We have already discovered amazing writers like Jill Malone, Sally Bellerose, and Hilary Sloin through the Bywater Prize. Which exciting new writer will we find next?

For more information about Bywater Books and the annual Bywater Prize for Fiction, please visit our website.

www.bywaterbooks.com